HARRY PUTTER
AND THE CHAMBER OF CHEESECAKES

BY
TIMOTHY R. O'DONNELL

CHAPTER ILLUSTRATIONS BY:
RILEY O'DONNELL, Age 9
GRIFFIN O'DONNELL, Age 11

COVER ILLUSTRATIONS BY:
TIMOTHY R. O'DONNELL

ISBN 1-4116-0688-4

Printed in the U.S.A.

THIS BOOK IS DEDICATED TO

RILEY AND GRIFFIN.

IT'S THEIR STORY TOO.

Contents

HARRY PUTTER

AND THE CHAMBER OF CHEESECAKES

Chapter 1

Cruel Summer

While most kids dream about being off from school, and find their summer to rocket by like a cheap amusement park ride, Harry Putter found summer to be the bane of his existence. It was because each summer found him at number 4 Privy Drive, living in the house he grew up in with his Aunt Hachooie, Uncle Vermin, and cousin Mudley, collectively known as the Dirtleys. Even though he was still spending this summer in the same place, it had started off with a bang, and had been like no other summer of his life.

Each summer Harry was treated like a subspecies. The Dirtleys didn't want Harry in their home, and resented his intrusion in their lives. In fact, from as early as he could remember he slept in the doghouse, literally, leaky roof and all. That is, until the summer after his first year of school. He came home and discovered the doghouse was gone. That summer he lived in the closet under the stairs. And even though Uncle Vermin squeezed a bed in there, Harry liked to sleep under it, rather than in it. He had grown accustomed to sleeping under his first bed ever, at school, for it seemed more like being in his old doghouse, only it didn't leak like his old doghouse. Harry thought he was in heaven, only a heaven where someone was trying to kill him. He thought Uncle Vermin was being nice, but later he found out that Hasbeen threatened to beat the snot out of his Uncle Vermin. Cubious Hasbeen was Harry's first friend ever, mostly because he always threatened to beat the snot out of his Uncle Vermin, but also because, he was the one who came and took Harry off to school changing his life forever. Being 1/32 part giant, Hasbeen was humongously fat and pretty intimidating, so the Dirtleys got rid of the doghouse to make appearances look good from the outside (in case Hasbeen should peek over the fence into the backyard), but not without a general increased resentment that they took out on Harry brutally. It wasn't until after his third year of school, that Harry came home to discover that he had a bedroom of his own. Uncle Vermin explained that the Tax Assessor had come by in the middle of that year, and was going to raise the property taxes because of the "added bedroom." Uncle Vermin had to get rid of Harry's bed to prove that it was really a closet, in order to avoid the additional taxes. So, Harry had his own room that summer, in the guestroom, a real bedroom, upstairs and everything. Of course, he still slept under the bed. But not this summer! This summer he slept in the master bedroom under a king-sized bed. Uncle Vermin and Aunt Hachooie had the guestroom.

Each summer Harry was treated like a slave. He had a list of chores a mile long. Some were difficult chores like, laundry, dishes, washing cars, scrubbing floors, sweeping chimneys, etc. Others were more menial, such as brushing Mudley's hair, plucking Uncle Vermin's nose hairs, or massaging Aunt Hachooie's bunioned feet.

He would come home from school and the place would look like it hadn't been cleaned for eight months. It was a pigsty that pigs wouldn't want to live in. (The Dirtleys of course, didn't seem to mind. They were just living up to their disgusting name.) He would spend each day cleaning until night when he would fall asleep exhausted. His only goals were to do a good job and thus avoid kicks to his ribs or the seat of his pants from the Dirtleys. Not this summer! This summer, he did no cleaning or chores.

Each summer Harry felt like he was slowly starving to death. Uncle Vermin rationed Harry's food and resented the cost of the little he spent to feed Harry. He sure mentioned it a lot. (Harry found it very surprising later in life that food and doghouses were a good deal less expensive than Uncle Vermin had him believe.) Harry was not allowed to be in the kitchen unobserved. All the work he did cooking and cleaning in the kitchen was conducted under the watchful eyes of Aunt Hachooie. He occasionally was able to sneak into the kitchen to steal something to eat, usually a handful of uncooked rice or macaroni. However, he always risked a thorough beating when doing so. This summer, Harry had developed a small spare tire on his slight frame.

In each of his past summers, Harry was forced to go to therapy sessions with the Dirtley's analyst for his supposed deep-seeded hatred of the Dirtleys. Though he tried several times, he was never able to convince his therapist that it was really the reverse, that the Dirtley's hated him. Nor did the analyst believe the fantastic stories that Harry told him: that he spent his early years sleeping in the doghouse; that he had a list of chores a mile long, or that he was being slowly starved to death– "Just look at me, I'm skin and bones!" Harry never mentioned any of his many adventures, or anything that really took place at school or else he would have been thrown in a straight jacket in a padded room. Once he had accidentally mentioned that his food talked to him, but was able to convince the therapist that he was only joking. This summer there were no therapy sessions.

Sure, this summer had started out exciting enough, but despite all the improvements, Harry Putter found himself bored. Today was too muggy outside, so Harry stayed in his room where the window air conditioner hummed and kept life bearable, another improvement realized only this summer.

He looked out of the window of his bedroom and sighed. All the neighborhood kids stayed far away from 4 Privy Drive even though

Uncle Vermin had a swimming pool installed in the backyard in April. They all had known for a long time that the weird kid with the L-shaped scar on his forehead lived there. Stay away from Harry Putter! It wouldn't have mattered anyway; the neighborhood kids were a bunch of morons the likes of which only his cousin Mudley could stomach. In fact, many of the sorry lot looked up to Mudley for leadership, a sorry lot indeed. That was fine with Harry, he wanted someone of intelligence to talk to, Ron, Hermione, heck he would settle for Neville Largebottom. But no one interesting was around, the only sign of life was the mailman heading from mailbox to mailbox delivering the mail, or as those in the wizarding community referred to it, the muddle mail. Muddle being the word they use for the poor humans that muddled through life without the use of magic. Wizards of course had a much more sophisticated mail delivery system.

Had the mailman looked up, he would have seen a skinny teenager with neat black hair and unibrow, wearing glasses that had been makeshift repaired with masking tape staring out of the window back down at him. Harry's hair was neat because he had Mudley brush it fifty-five strokes three times each day; he had a unibrow because it hurt too much when he had Mudley pluck the hairs growing between his eyebrows; and his glasses had been sat on by Hedbutt, his pet goat, that he loved more than anyone else in the world, besides himself.

But even Hedbutt was nowhere to be seen. Harry sighed again, flopped on the bed, and rummaged through a pile of comics. He considered the quibbage comic, The Adventures of the Furious Whacker, but settled on his copy of the latest Dr. Nova comic. However, he found himself only leafing through it with disinterest, he had read it three times already. He lay down on the bed and his eyes wandered around the room until he found himself staring at the Loose Cannons poster on the wall. The Loose Cannons were his favorite professional quibbage team. He sighed. The pool was boring, the neighborhood kids were boring, Nintendo was boring, even the comics were boring.

Even though he kept telling himself that it was the best summer of his entire life, and he had said so a half dozen times in letters to Ron and Hermione, who was he kidding? This summer was still the bane of his existence. It turned out that the ill treatment he had received from the Dirtleys was better than the constant boredom he endured this summer. What he really wished for was to be back at school, and he had a really bad school year last year, too. (No wonder everyone thought he had a severe case of stupid in the head.) However, school didn't start for three more days. And while Harry was happiest at school, it wasn't really his friends there that made him happy, certainly not the books and classes, after five years, six if you counted preschool, the magic held little magic for him. It wasn't even playing quibbage that made him happy. What Harry really wished for when he wished he were back at school, was for an adventure.

His protruding belly gave a pang, and Harry remembering the Reese's Peanut Butter Cups, decided to go downstairs and get a snack. He was quickly disappointed to find the empty package of Reese's contributing to an overall filthy kitchen counter stacked with used dishes and cups, an empty box of cereal, and a jug of milk someone had left out of the fridge all day, all on top of layers of other garbage. He picked up the wrapper and angrily thought to himself, "Mudley!" As he headed down the hallway past the closet under the stairs, and into the living room, he pulled out his magic wand and yelled, "Mudley Dirtley! You scumbucket! Where are you?"

In the living room, he spotted his Aunt Hachooie; she sat on the blue sofa with the doilies on the arms, near the air conditioner, frozen in the act of fanning herself, and with a look of fear and loathing on her gaunt face. Aunt Hachooie was a stern woman, tall and thin. She was very old fashioned in her thoughts and her appearance. She looked like she would keep a house just so. Not so, above all, she was a Dirtley, and that means trash. On top of that, she had grown accustomed to having Harry do all the real work keeping the house in order for so many years. Furthermore, she was used to commanding the Dirtley household like a tyrant, though Uncle Vermin didn't realize that he was not the one in charge. Harry immediately commanded her, "Go buy some more Reese's Peanut Butter Cups!" He jabbed his wand repeatedly, shooting off a few bolts of electricity from its tip to emphasize his words, and to get her moving, right quick.

"But …," said Aunt Hachooie, who was interrupted by the furiously crackling electrical bolts jolting her feet until her graying brown hair stood on end.

"Now!" shouted Harry. With several short cries, she danced from the room, out the front door, and ran to the car.

A whimper could be heard in the suddenly quiet living room. Harry turned and noticed Mudley's fat butt sticking out from behind the coffee table. Mudley chanced a peek over the edge of the table and quickly pulled his head back down as Harry set the coffee table ablaze with a fireball blast coming from his wand. Harry smiled with satisfaction at the piglike squeal that Mudley made. Mudley Dirtley was a big kid, who liked to throw his weight around. He had grown up teasing and bullying Harry. But ever since Harry had started using magic, he had moved on to terrorizing easier prey in the neighborhood. Mudley was a pig. In fact, there was pig blood in Mudley from his father's side of the family visible in his beady eyes, snout, and jowls.

Just then, a letter dropped through the slot in the front door. Harry knew right away that this letter was not the muddle mail. He opened the front door to confirm his suspicion, and saw the young goat that had delivered it scampering away. He sent a lightning bolt after the goat but missed, Aunt Hachooie leaving in the Dirtley's car, a mini Cooper, got in the way. He picked up the letter and tossed it on the burning coffee table where it quickly shriveled to ashes in the blaze. He had gotten so many of these letters so far this summer, (in reality a hundred and fifty seven) that he could recite them by heart.

"The use of all methods of magical incantation, enchantment, and summoning by any 1st through 6th year students outside of Hogwashes school for Witchcraft and Wizardry is strictly forbidden and most definitely not allowed. Desist immediately in using magic in the presence of muddles.

The Department of Wizard Affairs"

Harry scoffed at the idea that some silly rule that was meant for unimportant children, who might do something dangerous using magic without supervision, might somehow apply to the great Harry Putter. Preposterous!

The warning notice also reminded Harry of the excitement of the very beginning of summer. There had been another big trial, Harry's second. (In his first trial Harry got off using a temporary insanity plea.) The Ministry of Magic really thought they had him this time, when he began using his magic on his first day back from school to educate the Dirtleys on what Harry called the New House Order.

The Ministry had tried to seize his wand that day, but Harry wouldn't relinquish it. He sent the Ministry's lackey scurrying back to the Ministry without his own wand, let alone Harry's. Next, the Ministry sent over an Auditor, a wizard who is adept in the magical field of Accounting. An Auditor uses accounting practices to stun their quarry, until dumbfounded, they submit to paying taxes, interest penalties, and worst of all are beguiled into letting the Auditor prepare their financial and tax reports. Harry was greatly relieved when the Ministry sent over Kingsley Shuckthecorn to audit him. Kingsley was a member of The Order of the Harry Putter Fan Club, and according to club bylaws, was not allowed to take Harry's wand. Kingsley was forced to resign his lucrative Ministry position at once, and immediately helped Harry to defend himself against any further Ministry attempts.

Caramelly Fudge, the Minister of Magic, was furious! He hated Harry Putter. Harry was alive, famous, and loved, while his own son, Maple-Walnut, had died while imprisoned in Azcabanana, notoriously infamous. He wanted Harry to die likewise. So next, he ordered a hundred of The Demented to bring Harry and the rogue Auditor Shuckthecorn in. The Demented wear black robes, which according to all rules automatically makes them bad guys. Many that they visit become uncomfortable when they notice their skeletal hands and the black hoods that hide their numbskulls. Their presence cause a variety of reactions from those whom they visit, ranging from hysterical screaming to hysterical laughter, to hiding under the sofa. An awful lot of them start a sentence that begins, "What the..." Many have grim feelings, or feelings of regret when they notice the large scythes that all The Demented carry. Some get a feeling their time has come to an end, and see their lives flash before their eyes. Some die right then and there. But few know what makes them really scary. The kiss of The Demented causes premature hair loss.

When Caramelly Fudge ordered The Demented to bring Harry and Kingsley in, it was because he remembered how much Harry feared them. Harry was very fond of his lustrous full head of hair, because he felt it was his best feature. However, Caramelly Fudge had forgotten that Harry had already overcome his fear and defeated The Demented on several occasions. Harry knew how to patronize them, and The Demented could not stand to be patronized, it was their only weakness. When they showed up, Harry dismissed them with a wave of his hand, not acknowledge them or their scariness for a second. They left feeling very dejected.

Caramelly Fudge was not finished yet. He cleared his schedule, and ordered a trial for that Friday. Harry Putter was going to face the music, and it would be a full trial, with a bench of nine judges. He, himself, would oversee the whole thing as the Chief Justice. By Thursday, the whole Ministry of Magic was practically patting themselves on the back, with the exception of Arthur Cheesley, the father of Harry's best friend, Ron, and a big Harry Putter fan. (Arthur Cheesley had a huge collection of Harry Putter apparel and toys.) When word of the trial reached him in the Department of Muddle Artifacts, he immediately rushed over to the Dirtley House. Apparently, his way of keeping Harry calm about the trial was to pace around saying over and over, "What are we going to do?" No matter how many times Harry told him not to worry about it, he just couldn't stop. Harry finally had to call Mrs. Cheesley to take him home.

The rest of the ministry was happily excited; they were finally going to nail that impudent delinquent, Harry Putter on something. They didn't really care what it was, just as long as they were able to lock him away in Azcabanana Prison, the prison for wizards.

When Friday came, Caramelly Fudge was beaming with delight as he donned his judges robes. It was going to be a great day! When the court bailiff announced him, he marshaled into the courtroom pompously. He took his seat among the eight other judges, all his puppets, and smiled wickedly down from the ridiculously high bench at the boy. A good sign that the boy showed up, he had secretly been wondering what he would do if he hadn't. Better still, the boy was alone, as planned. Harry had shown up because he was bored, and thought the trial might pass the day. He had heard prisoners get three square meals a day, and he found it amusing that he was tempted to try it out. He seriously doubted that Azcabanana Prison could be any worse than living with the Dirtleys.

But in all seriousness, he doubted that he'd have the kind of adventures that he really enjoyed at school, if he were imprisoned, so he had no intention of allowing them to throw him in the wizard jail.

The trial was being held in the same courtroom that his previous trial had taken place in, however, it was even dustier than last time. He doubted it had been used since. He sat in his chair feeling very small in front of the row of judges that stared down at him like an accusation.

Judge Fudge began, "Mr. Putter, I notice that your counsel is absent today, where's Grumblesnore?"

"I dunno," shrugged Harry.

Fudge tittered to himself, for he knew very well where Elvis Grumblesnore was. Professor Grumblesnore, the schoolmaster of Hogwashes, was on the sixth floor of that very building. He would be answering a barrage of Auditor questions for the rest of the day. Fudge had arranged the whole thing. Grumblesnore won't get you off the hook this time!

"Oh, that's too bad, he frowned, "but we can't reschedule the trial, we're very busy you know."

To this comment Perky Cheesley, the court transcriptionist, laughed until his nose turned brown. Perky Cheesley was the estranged brother of Harry's friend Ron. He was also Caramelly Fudge's adoring underling. Perky Cheesley was a huge moron in many ways and somehow had gotten hooked on Caramelly Fudge, and wanted nothing more than to have Caramelly Fudge like him, and if that meant hating Harry Putter too, so be it. Perky could do that. His father, Arthur Cheesley had disowned him for it. To Arthur, liking Caramelly Fudge was bad enough, but disliking Harry Putter well, that was going against the family! In fact, Arthur wished Harry was family, almost as much as he wished Perky wasn't. The whole Cheesley family are card-carrying members of The Order of the Harry Putter Fan Club, except Perky. The rest of the judges continued to scowl down at Harry as if he was a war criminal.

"Let's see," said Fudge as though he weren't intimately familiar with the case, "you have been sent, oh dear, how many? I can't count them all. Forty-seven warning notices for the use of magic by a sixth year student, and in the presence of muddles!" He put a note of shocking appall in his voice. "How can this be, school has been out only one week! What's this? Refused to relinquish his wand! Tsk, Tsk! Attacked ministry personnel! Subverted ministry personnel! And patronized The Demented! Harry Putter, have you no shame? What ever has become of the good little boy, I once knew? It can't be true! There must be some mistake! Eh, how do you plead?"

"Not Guilty."

"What?" Fudge let slip. He couldn't believe this hoodlum had the audacity to plead Not Guilty.

"Not Guilty," Harry repeated a good deal louder.
After a moment to collect his thoughts, Fudge said, "Right, well, let's get this young man sworn in shall we?"

The bailiff had Harry put his hand in the Thumbscrew of Truth or Ulp. Then asked Harry, "Do you swear to tell the truth, the whole truth, and nothing but the truth so help you or else, Ulp?"

Harry was nervous now, his voice cracked when he said, "I-I do." The magic thumbscrew began to glow with a soft blue light, and rotated to a point of discomfort. Harry knew that any lies would cause the Thumbscrew of Truth or Ulp to tighten unmercifully; the pain would be excruciating, and the lie would be obvious to all who viewed his writhing pain. Harry had no choice but to tell the truth.

Caramelly Fudge smiled his wicked smile again, and began. "You are Harry Putter of 4 Privy Drive?"

"Y-y-yes."

"And you are a student at Hogwashes School for Witchcraft and Wizardry?"

"Yes."

"And how long has school been in recess this summer?"

"Since last Friday. One week."

"And since last Friday, have you used magic?" Fudge peered closely at Harry.

"Yes."

"Ah ha! And how many times have you used magic?"

"I don't know, dozens of times." To Harry's relief the thumbscrew didn't automatically tighten when he didn't know the precise answer, just as long as he told the truth he would be fine.

"And have you received any warning notices regarding the use of magic during your recess?'

"Yes."

"And you understand what those warnings mean?"

"Yes."

"Oh really? It doesn't seem to me you did!" Fudge looked around the bench, and received the laughter from this statement that he felt it deserved.

"So, after receiving the warnings, you continued to perform magic? Is that correct?"

"Yes."

"A total of forty seven times this past week?"

Harry was worried that this question was a trap. He had lost count of how many times he had used magic on the Dirtleys, and was indeed a bit surprised that it was so often. If he said yes, and it was the wrong amount, would the Thumbscrew tighten? Drops of sweat began to bead on his forehead. He replied, "If you say so, Sir."

"Yes, I do say so. You received forty-seven warning notices, and ignored them all! In fact, didn't a ministry authority come to collect your wand?"

"Yes."

"And did you use magic on him?"

"Yes."

"Instead of relinquishing your own wand, you captured his, did you not?"

"I did."

"And you sent him packing didn't you?"

"I did."

"Shameful! Is that how you treat representatives of the ministry?"

"Yes, I did."

"And afterward, the Ministry of Magic sent an Auditor to collect your wand, did you use magic on him?"

"No."

Fudge paused a bit confused. He expected that the Thumbscrew of Truth or Ulp would have the boy writhing for his last answer. "Bailiff, is that Thumbscrew in working order?"

The bailiff stepped forward, and said, "It passed its morning check, was working fine."

"Test it again," Fudge ordered.

The bailiff removed the Thumbscrew of Truth or Ulp from Harry, and placed it on his own hand. "I swear to tell the truth, the whole truth, and nothing but the truth or else, Ulp."

Then the bailiff braced himself and said, "I love my mother-in-law!" He was quickly thrashing around in agony. In a panic, he began shouting, "I hate her! I can't stand her. I hate my mother-in-law!" His pain subsided.

"It's workin' just fine!" The bailiff removed the device, and swore Harry back in.

"Shall we continue?" Fudge cleared his voice. "The Ministry of Magic sent an Auditor to collect your wand, did you use magic on him?"

"No."

Fudge frowned, disappointed. He did not know how Harry could have subverted the Auditor without magic, but, no matter, he had

Harry Putter right where he wanted him. The boy had admitted under oath to using magic forty-seven times during the first week of summer recess! It was an open and shut case. He would wrap it up very soon.

"Fine. The ministry then sent The Demented to collect you and your wand, did you use magic on The Demented?"

"No."

Fudge scowled. "So, you have admitted to using magic forty-seven times this week! Yet, for some reason, you chose to plea, 'Not Guilty!' Were you confused about the meaning of Not Guilty?"

"No, Sir."

"Quite right! You pleaded Not Guilty because you thought you could weasel your way out it, like you did last trial!"

"No, Sir."

"Well then, would you like to change your plea to Guilty then?"

"No, Sir."

Caramelly Fudge rapped his gavel and stood up. He was infuriated. "What are you saying Harry Putter? That you are Not Guilty after you have already admitted in front of all of us that you are!"

"No, Sir."

"'No, Sir?'"

"The law states, 'The use of all methods of magical incantation, enchantment, and summoning by any 1st through 6th year students outside of Hogwashes School for Witchcraft and Wizardry is strictly forbidden and most definitely not allowed,'" quoted Harry. "However, this rule doesn't apply to me."

"No one is above the law, Harry Putter!" Fudge raised his voice. "I am very disappointed in you, boy. Just because you are a celebrity of sorts, does not mean you will be treated differently in the eyes of this court! Justice is blind!"

"That's not what I mean, Sir."

"No? But you say this rule doesn't apply to you? How so?"

"The law applies to students from their 1st year through their 6th year. After six years of school, any student is old enough to use magic at home. In fact, most students, after six years, are encouraged to begin to use magic to help out around the house, doing dishes, cooking, straightening up."

"But the school records show that you will be entering your sixth year this autumn, Harry. You just took your G.O.A.T. tests, did you not?"

"Yes, Sir."

"See then, you have only completed five years of school! I'm sorry Harry, this law does apply to you, and ignorance is no excuse!"

"Not so, Sir, I have completed six years of school, if you count preschool, which of course I always do."

At this comment, the eight judges began to whisper to each other excitedly. Fudge rapped his gavel for silence.

"Silly boy. Preschool doesn't count!"

"Yes, it does."

"Preschool is a farce, Harry, you only go to preschool when your parents don't want you around. Which explains why YOU attended preschool, doesn't it."

"Sir, my parents were dead, it's my aunt and uncle who didn't want me around."

"That's besides the point, no one counts preschool. Preschool doesn't count!"

"Sir, if you check the law, nowhere does it say that preschool doesn't count. Furthermore, I can prove that it does count."

"You can?"

"Yes."

And even though, the Ministry tried very hard to not count preschool, it didn't take much to legally prove that preschool does, in fact, count. Harry was able to prove that the most important lessons in life are in fact taught in preschool, such as: if it's anything good, the answer is "No;" adding water balloons to any given situation is generally a bad idea; girls under 12 are icky and have cooties; pants are generally not considered optional; and that the world would be a better place if we all took a nap in the afternoon.

Furthermore, Hogwashes records, that were conveniently in the building as Grumblesnore was attempting to answer the Auditor's inquisition, clearly showed that the school charged the same rate for preschool as it did any other year of school. Harry proved that preschool counted from a learning perspective, it counted from a business perspective, and it was not legally different from any other year of school. The Ministry of Magic had no recourse but to let Harry go, and rewrite the laws, which would take a very long time, as the Department of Wizard Affairs is in many ways slower than the British parliamentary system. Why it was almost the end of summer, and they still hadn't managed to stop sending the automatic warning notices by goat post.

Harry had foiled them yet again.

He snapped out of his reverie, Mudley was gone. Harry wasn't feeling quite as angry anyway. Uncle Vermin had come into the living room, waddling in from the kitchen with the fire extinguisher. Uncle Vermin was a large neckless man, with a purple complexion that made him look like he was long overdue for a massive heart attack. He was surprisingly calm considering his coffee table was ablaze. Harry almost didn't notice the peanut butter cup sticking out of Uncle Vermin's mouth, –almost. As Uncle Vermin let loose with the fire extinguisher, Harry gave him a kick in the pants. "Eat the last Reese's? I oughta get my friends over here to teach you a lesson, you fat lard! You remember my friends, don't you?" Harry was of course referring to his friends in The Order of the Harry Putter Fan Club, who had escorted him home after school last June.

They had given Uncle Vermin a stern warning not to mistreat Harry. There was Mad Dog Hooty, Frommundigus Filcher, Kingsley Shuckthecorn, Wrestlemania Trunks, Rhomulus Loopin, and Fabulous Butterpants. All diehard Harry Putter fans, they spent most of their time discussing and debating the trivial details of Harry Putter's many adventures, and knew everything about Harry. They were very useful at times and completely overprotective of their idol. All Harry had to do was send a note by goat, and his friends would storm the house, and give his Uncle the thrashing of his life. He wasn't sure that they wouldn't end up killing Uncle Vermin. Harry didn't want that, and really hadn't needed their help so far this summer.

"Oh, yes, Harry, but I ...." started Uncle Vermin.

"You know the one with that evil eyeball? He's an escaped killer and head of the wizard mafia." Harry embellished Mad Dog Hooty's reputation. In reality, Mad Dog Hooty did have an evil eyeball, was the world's greatest Auditor, and had the scars to prove it, though now he was retired.

"Yes, but ...." started Uncle Vermin again.

"Give me one good reason why I shouldn't call my friends here to lay some Serious Smack down on you!" said Harry getting himself worked up again.

Serious Smack was his Uncle and godfather. A pang of regret seized Harry, using his dead uncle's name, for he had only met his uncle once, briefly. Harry had wanted desperately to get to know his Uncle Serious, however, his uncle seemed to desperately not want to get to know Harry. He managed to escape Harry the one time Harry met him, had eluded his every attempt to meet him after that, and had unfortunately died recently. All Harry had to remind him of the uncle he never knew was his John Deere 2000 lawnmower. Serious Smack had given it to Harry as a bribe. He sent it to Harry one Christmas with a note asking Harry to take the lawnmower, leave him alone, and stop trying to find him. Harry couldn't help himself; he kept the lawnmower and kept trying to locate his uncle. In the end, Serious Smack died suddenly in a bizarre circus tragedy while trying to escape from Harry. It was all Harry's fault that his uncle was dead. If only he hadn't pushed, hadn't persistently kept trying to find him, he would still be alive today. However, Uncle Vermin didn't know he was dead, and was more scared of Serious Smack then all Harry's other weird friends combined. Serious Smack was a clown, and Uncle Vermin was very afraid of clowns.

"There is a whole 'nother package of Reese's in the cupboard," replied Uncle Vermin both a little smug and a little afraid that Harry might be insulted by his smugness.

"Oh," he blinked repeatedly. "Well then, bring me some and some chocolate milk, too."

A little later Harry was outside relaxing by the pool in a chaise lounge. He ate his snack while reading his quibbage comic again. He noticed the ad in it for the latest Spiderman comic, and became annoyed. It reminded him that he didn't get the subscription to Spiderman that he had asked for as a birthday present. It was just one more thing that the Dirtleys did wrong this summer. When Aunt Hachooie came outside with a new package of peanut butter cups, she had sweat on her brow. Harry said, "Thanks, can you be a dear and run out and get me the latest Spiderman comic? It just came out yesterday."

Aunt Hachooie sighed as she headed back out again, reciting her mantra to herself, "Only three more days.... only three more days...."

Harry decided to go inside and play some Nintendo. On the way in, another goat showed up, this one was much bigger and older.

The goat had a letter in its mouth, which Harry grabbed, thinking, "What now?"

He noticed the official Hogwashes seal and opened it immediately. His jaw dropped as he read it. Finally saying aloud in disbelief to no one but himself, "School has been canceled?"

Chapter 2

Conspiracy

"Something can't be right. Hogwashes can't close!"

What could have happened to cause school to be closed this year? Was Grumblesnore in trouble? Was Caramelly Fudge somehow behind this? Harry still couldn't believe it. No matter how much better this summer had been compared to every summer he had ever had before, no matter how much fun it was torturing the Dirtleys both physically and mentally, he was still greatly looking forward to going back to school, seeing his friends, just being where he belonged, and of course having another adventure. He and his fans expected no less. He folded the letter and put it in the back pocket of his jeans, which were incidentally about four inches shorter than they should have been, and decided that if it was still there later, then this couldn't be just a bad dream.

In the den, he absentmindedly turned on the television. Some commercial was on for breakfast cereal. He switched on the Nintendo, changed the channel to 4 and started playing Zombie King II, Die Again Evil Dead. Suddenly, the same stupid elf hawking breakfast cereal was there again in the middle of his game. When most commercials had music and lots of loud talking, this one was strangely silent. All he could hear was the background music to Zombie King II. He took a closer look. It looked a lot like Bobby

the elf, but wearing a box of cereal instead of clothes. Elves naturally didn't wear clothes, clothes being a human convention. However, those that served humans usually attempt to attire in something, as humans tend to stare, making them feel naked when they are naked. Elves typically are not very particular in what they choose to wear. Kitchen-Elves generally wear empty sacks of flour, Laboratory-Elves sometimes wear rubber gloves, and Shoemaking-Elves typically wear old socks. However, Elves do wear uniforms if required by their masters, and a lot of them do like to have their elven servants dressed in a manner that reflects tastefully on the households they serve.

"Is this some kind of commercial?" Harry asked perplexed.

The elf in the cereal box timidly spoke up, "Hello, Harry Putter, Sir. This is a public service announcement. Ahem, Hogwashes School of Witchcraft and Wizardry regrets to inform you that school is canceled until further notice."

It was Bobby the elf.

Three years ago, Harry had accidentally gotten Bobby enslaved. There are very few jobs that Free-Elves are willing to do, and Bobby had been very fortunate to be happily employed by the Maldoy family. Respectable wizardly households are difficult to find, and the Maldoys are highly regarded as one of the best, if not the best family to work for. Free-elves are not paid as part of their employment as they have no use for wizard currency. Elves value magical power, and the Maldoys had it. They are one of the most powerful wizard families in terms of magic, and thus the most enviable of families for elves to work for. The Cheesleys, on the other hand, attract no elves to their household, as their magical power is even collectively rather, well let's just say, it's a good thing their house has electricity. The long-term proximity to a good magical family creates a symbiosis from which both the family and the Free-Elf benefit greatly. The Free-Elf benefits by absorbing magical power from those he serves, while his service, in return makes the family's magical equipment, laboratory equipment, and magical devices operate smoothly. The wizard family with a Free-Elf servant finds it easier to concentrate, their potions are stronger, and their magic more efficient through the elf's freely given service. Thus, Bobby was greatly respected among the Free-Elves, and his opinion was highly sought after, especially regarding matters of good taste, particularly regarding clothing. But Bobby was no longer a Free-Elf, thanks to none other than Harry Putter.

The sudden event that enslaved Bobby happened accidentally during Harry's second year at Hogwashes, right after he had found the Chamber of Frozen Dairy Desserts and rescued those who had gotten brainfreezed including his good friend Hermione, but most of all Ginny Cheesley. Ginny, the sister of Harry's good friend Ron, had been kidnapped and taken to the Chamber of Frozen Dairy Desserts by the persevering spirit of Tom Riddly. Harry found the hidden chamber, defeated a giant mildew stain, and prevented Riddly from coming back to life by destroying the only copy of his Frozen Dairy Dessert Cookbook.

At the conclusion of his adventure, Harry's feet had gotten wet in the fight versus the giant mildew stain, he was after all knee deep in mildew. When he slogged into Elvis Grumblesnore's office to return a few bleach-based household cleaners that he had borrowed during his battle, he found himself interrupting a conversation with Grumblesnore and Luscious Maldoy, who was there along with his Free-Elf servant, Bobby. Luscious was there in the capacity of chairman of the Hogwashes Board of Education. It was therefore his duty to relieve Grumblesnore of his position as the school's headmaster. Grumblesnore was being relieved of his duties because of the danger the Chamber of Frozen Dairy Deserts represented to the student body, and most of all for his ineptitude in locating the chamber and closing it forever. That's when Harry informed them both that he had found the Chamber and closed it forever, and presented the tattered remains of the Frozen Dairy Dessert Cookbook as evidence. Luscious Maldoy was quite miffed. Harry thought he was doing a great service, saving his good friend and mentor, Grumblesnore's job, but Grumblesnore was quite miffed too. The idea of an early retirement was very appealing to him, especially in light of all his recent troubles, the beginning of which coincided with Harry's arrival at Hogwashes.

It was at this point that Harry, could no longer stand the wetness of his socks and inconsiderately removed them. Well, on a good day, Harry's feet stank; on a bad day, his feet were like a stink bomb that induced coughing, dizziness, and watery eyes. That day, the dampness of his shoes along with the giant mildew stain remnants that had seeped into his shoes and socks somehow reacted very unfavorably with Harry's feet. When he removed his shoes, his socks went off like a concussion grenade, sending a shockwave through the building. Grumblesnore and Luscious were stunned. Bobby went into immediate cardiac arrest. The elf was going to kick the bucket, when Grumblesnore scooped him up, and fled for St. Mongo's Hospital for the Magically Afflicted. (This was no job for the school nurse, Ms. Pomfrite.) How Grumblesnore was able to break his momentary shock and to summon the stamina to get Bobby out of there and away, is a mystery of superhuman effort. He collapsed a moment later there in the hospital. By comparison, Luscious Maldoy fell unconscious and was not rescued until emergency workers in Hazmat suits arrived. Harry, of course, was immune to his own stench.

But that course of events, in a nutshell, is what made Bobby a slave. For elves, it is no small thing, the act of saving their lives, as it is with most humans. It is their custom, when someone saves their lives, to devote the remainder of their lives from that moment forward to their rescuer as his slave. There are countless examples, such as St. Nicholas when he rescued an entire village of elves from being bulldozed by the East Millstone Condominium Construction

Company, or Brian Keebler, the lumberjack who rescued a whole tree full of elves from a woodpecker one day.

Ever since that fateful day, Bobby has served Grumblesnore faithfully as his slave. He adores Grumblesnore as his savior, and would gladly give his own life in exchange for Grumblesnore's life, if the opportunity ever presented itself. However, should he ever actually save Grumblesnore's life, he would then become a Free-Elf once again.

Ever since that fateful day, Bobby hated Harry Putter. In the three years since, Bobby had made countless failed attempts on Harry's life, and he often conspired with others who were also trying to kill Harry. Bobby pretended to be Harry's friend in order to lure him into traps, as he had tried on several occasions. After several attempts to kill Harry failed miserably, yet clearly involved the elf, it became suddenly clear to Harry that Bobby was trying to kill him. Harry couldn't blame him, he felt terribly responsible about Bobby's enslavement even though it had been an accident. So, Harry never let on that he knew Bobby was in fact his enemy. He pretended to be friends with Bobby, just as Bobby pretended to be his friend.

It was bad enough that Harry was responsible for Bobby's enslavement, yet there was one other important incident that caused Bobby to hate Harry Putter even more. Harry was also responsible for one other terrible sin that Bobby couldn't forgive. Harry had gotten Bobby's elf friend, Binky, fired from her noble position as the Free-Elf servant to none other than the reputable Bartimous Grouch. Though she remained a Free-Elf, she was shamed. Binky was perhaps looked upon as even lower than a Slave-Elf, because she had gotten sacked, something that hadn't happened to a Free-Elf in over three thousand years.

It happened two years ago at the World Tea Cup Tournament. Bobby had put another of his schemes into effect by launching a Fungus Eater mark into the sky. The terrifying mark, a mushroom, which had not been seen for years, indicated that the Fungus Eaters were back. It had the same effect on the various privileged members of the wizarding community there at the World Tea Cup Tournament that launching a firework into the sky indicating that Disco was alive and well today would have on a crowd of muddles at a sporting event, –mass hysteria. People were fleeing for their lives. However, there were many brave people out searching the grounds and nearby woods looking for the culprit, including Harry.

As it turned out, Harry was the first one to find Bobby holding the bazooka-like firework launcher. Harry asked Bobby what he had. Bobby lied, explaining that he had found it in the grass, and handed it innocently to Harry. Bobby, let out an evil laugh, then quickly disappeared, leaving Harry literally holding the smoking gun. It looked like Harry was going to take the blame for the whole incident; he was holding the launcher, his fingerprints were on the gun. He had to do something fast, before he was found, or else Bobby would have succeeded in framing Harry for the despicable deed. Harry would be thrown in Azcabanana Prison to languish miserably the rest of his life, surrounded by The Demented. Harry heard voices coming his way, and panicking, he threw the launcher over some nearby bushes, where it landed on Bobby's elf friend, Binky's head. Binky crawled out of the bushes holding the launcher right in front of her master, Bartimous Grouch, Arthur Cheesley, Caramelly Fudge, Harry and two Auditors. It was Binky who ended up taking the fall, and losing her desirable position and her respectability. Ironically, Bobby blamed that no good, tricky, Harry (he'll pay for this!) Putter, for the whole incident.

"Come on, Bobby, school is canceled this year? You can't expect me to believe this, do you?" asked Harry.

"Oh darn, you figured out Bobby's little trick, school isn't really closed, but there is something that is very serious, Sir! Bobby, at great risk to his own life, is here to warn you of great danger!" said

Bobby lowering his voice, and pressing his nose against the inside glass of the television screen. He seemed afraid someone might overhear him, but Harry rolled his eyes, he knew that it was all an act. Bobby was setting up his next bumbling attempt on Harry's life.

"Now? I'm in the middle of killing zombies, that is, if you don't mind getting out of the way!" replied Harry starting to get annoyed.

"Oh, no, Sir! You are in immense danger," whispered the elf.

"Don't be silly, I think I can take the Zombie King down."

"That's not what I mean, Sir! Bobby means if you go to school this year, you will surely perish!" said Bobby dramatically.

Harry flopped back on the couch and scoffed, "The past five years, six if you count preschool, which I always do, someone has tried to kill me, and I've escaped every time. So what's so dangerous this time?"

"You are in far greater danger this time, Sir! This time there is a conspiracy to kill you. Everyone wants you dead!" exaggerated the cereal box clad elf.

"Come on, Bobby! Everyone? What about all my friends? They don't want me dead."

"They will after they find out you cheated to win all those quibbage matches!"

Harry jumped to his feet. "What! I never cheated!"

"Yes, that's true, Sir, but once they read those letters saying that you cheated, they will . . ."

Harry interrupted, "Letters? What letters?"

"The letters Bobby sent out last night to your friends and teachers. They should have received them this morning, Sir."

Infuriated, Harry put his foot through the television into Bobby's face with a satisfying crash of broken glass and crunch of broken tooth. The elf groaned, "Ow, thank you, Sir, I deserve that and more for the terrible things Bobby has done. Please do it again!" This time he was ready to catch Harry's foot and bite his ankle.

"But why? Why did you send those letters?" asked Harry angrily.

"Well, as I said, Sir, there is a conspiracy to do you in this year, once and for all."

"So who is the head of this conspiracy? And why are you helping them?" demanded Harry.

Oh, I cannot name him, Sir!" replied the elf.

"Just as I thought! He-Who-Must-Not-Be-Smelled! Lord Moldyfart!" deduced Harry.

Lord Moldyfart was the nemesis of Harry Putter. He was his enemy even before Harry was born. All because of a dreadful prophecy that Moldyfart had learned about back when he was known as young Tom Farisol Riddly. Tom found the prophecy when he opened a Chinese fortune cookie at the New China Kitchen in South London. He cracked it open and read his fortune, "Someone in your future will steal your heart." Tom who was always paranoid, freaked out. He clenched the tiny slip of paper in his fist and thought, "Who is this mysterious enemy, and why would he try to steal my heart, especially when I'm not finished with it!" It made him furious.

Tom Riddly used this prophesized enemy as motivation to become the most powerful and ruthless sorcerer he could be. When his future enemy arrived, he would be ready. It became his life long obsession. He made two vows. The first, that when the one who would try to steal his heart came, he wouldn't give the poor fool a chance, he would tear him apart. He would not allow laws or emotions to get in the way of his defenses. He would break the wizarding laws, use unforgettable curses, if they would give him an advantage over his unknown foe. The second, that he wouldn't eat Chinese food ever again.

Over the years, his heart became a stone, such that none could steal it, no seed of love could find purchase to grow. For he had no thoughts of love, his burning desire was to be ready when his enemy arrived. He could harbor no weakness, for his enemy might use it against him. Love was for the weak. He closed his heart to all humankind, for, his enemy could be anyone, and so he trusted no one. Incidentally, he had ignored a young girl at the library, who had flirted with him to get his attention on several occasions. Had his obsession not been all encompassing, he might have noticed her, she may have even stolen his heart, as it was, she ended up marrying Arthur Cheesley. The young girl in the library was Molly Cheesley, and to this day, has a slight crush on Tom Riddly that she has kept secret all these years.

Riddly, not satisfied with his expertise in standard magic and even illegal magic, eventually began to practice dark magic, and learned everything he could. In his malignant studies, he did his own research and taught himself, until his understanding surpassed the dark knowledge of any living wizard. In doing so, he became the most powerful wizard alive, but at great cost, for had given up his own humanity.

During his research he had consorted with penguins, demons, and llamas and learned what he could from them, and he made some deals that were costly. The unholy pacts he made changed his true form. He used his sorcery to hide the creature that he had become, so that he still looked like a man, but was something else entirely, something without a heart, something that couldn't die, for no man knew the one word of power that would change him back to his true form where he would be vulnerable to death. Only one demon knew the word, and Tom destroyed that demon and ate its soul. He was more than the most terrible wizard the world had ever known; he was invincible.

His true countenance was a horror that men shrank from. Why even the odors he made were powerful enough to kill flowers and small animals, and strike fear into any living man. He had reached the pinnacle of his power and repulsion. It was at this point that he decided to rearrange the letters of his name, Tom Farisol Riddly, to spell "I is Lord Moldyfart." It was a name more suited to a being of his awfulness, a name that people would fear to speak, lest the Fart Lord harken to their unwanted call, and answer like a spoken doom.

He was ready for his enemy, and still his unknown enemy did not come. He began to fear that his hideous reputation had preceded him, scaring his foe away. Then it occurred to him that if he could find out who his enemy was, perhaps he could find and destroy his foe, possibly while he or she was weak and unready to face his mighty wrath. He cared not whether his enemy was a man, woman, or child. He made a new vow. He swore that he would find out who his enemy was, and kill him. He would seek out and destroy his enemy without mercy.

Sitting in the lotus position, he relaxed his body, closed his eyes, and momentarily attained inner peace. When he was ready, he summoned his power, focusing his ethereal perception. He used his summoned alternate awareness to glean and unravel the veil that kept the future unseen by all but those few with extraordinary gifts. He located and followed the dark thread that represented his own life, through the tangled myriad of intersections. He noticed that it soon tangled with a silver thread, and suspected that this was the thread of his enemy's life. He continued to follow his own dark thread, complexly intertwined with the silver one, until he found that the silver one cut his own life's thread off at its very end. Then he was certain this silver thread was the thread of his enemy. The thread shined with a goodness and innocence that made him furious. He longed to yank it from the fabric of time, and rid himself of it, however, the thread was too tangled with his own. Any pressure at all might cut his own thread at the same time, or worse still, instead of the silver one. He dared not. Sneering as he followed the silver thread back to its start, he discovered the date, time, and place of his enemy's birth, July 31, 1989, 7 pm, London. He laughed as he returned to his own consciousness. His enemy was but an infant. He had no scruples about killing a child.

Further research showed that two children were born on July 31, 1989 at 7 pm in London, one was a boy named Harry Putter, born to James and Lillyput Putter. The other was a boy named Neville Largebottom, born to Jumbo and Begonia Largebottom. Moldyfart would kill both infants.

That night Moldyfart planned to visit two households. He attacked the Putter household first. He slaughtered James and Lillyput Putter as they tried to save their infant son, Harry. Their magic was nothing when compared to his own, they died a horrible death. Then Moldyfart picked up the infant from his crib. The baby smiled, then spit up on him. However, that was the least of Moldyfart's worries. For at that moment he discovered that his new form wasn't quite as invulnerable as the demon that had sold it to him had made it out to be. Moldyfart had a rather bad reaction to the Ivory Snow detergent that Harry's parents used to wash his footed pajamas. The pureness of the Ivory Snow was a bane to Moldyfart's impure life form. He found himself rapidly as vulnerable as he thought the infant, whom he could no longer hold in his arms, was but a moment ago. The child fell, hitting his forehead on the corner of the crib, leaving an "L"-shaped wound. Moldyfart's powers were gone, he was shriveling up like a slug on the sidewalk in the sun. Yet he could not die. "Oh, darn," he thought as he slinked away. For a very long time, he lay in a hole in the ground very close to death, wishing for death, yet unable to die. It would take years for him to recover. He renewed his vows, one day, he would kill Harry Putter, and he would never eat Chinese food again.

And indeed, Lord Moldyfart did try several times to kill Harry Putter even when he was not at his full strength. Yet somehow his adversary had eluded his every attempt, and in some cases had even caused severe setbacks to Moldyfart's recovery. However,

Moldyfart had finally managed to return to his full power a year ago, and while Harry may have proven his foot odor was a match for Moldyfart's power, stench for stench, Moldyfart had other powers that he hoped to test against his enemy soon.

Harry knew his real enemy, Moldyfart, had only begun to fight, and would be at the crux of any conspiracy to kill him.

"Well, you know how it is, Sir, sixth time's the charm! Really seventh time if you include preschool." replied Bobby, relieved that he had not been revealed the true leader of the conspiracy, and hadn't answered Harry's second question (Why are you helping him?) at all.

"Hmmm, I think I know how to solve this problem," said Harry more to himself than to Bobby.

"How, Sir?" inquired the elf.

"Well, Moldyfart obviously wants me to go to school, because you are trying to convince me not to go. He knows I will not listen to you, and go to school anyway, just like I always do. And then this conspiracy of his will do me in. He probably has planted several Fungus Eaters inside Hogwashes, while I've been sitting around on my butt enjoying the summer! Now that I've figured out his little scheme, I can easily thwart it. Ha, Ha! I'm going to take a year off from school!" laughed Harry.

Having adventures was one thing, fighting a well-planned conspiracy to kill you, well, Harry would just as soon skip that. He was happy that he would have a nice long vacation from the toil of school work as well as the inevitable danger to his person he had experienced at Hogwashes the past five years, six if you counted preschool. They really needed to get some better security over there. He would have to talk to Grumblesnore about it. Then he laughed again, he wasn't going to be seeing Grumblesnore for a year!

He grabbed Bobby by the neck, pulled him out of the broken television, and tossed the elf out of the window.

"Thank you, Sir," came the elf's receding voice.

Chapter 3

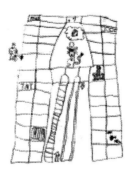

Abis Mall

The next day Harry was to meet Ron and Hermione at the Abis Mall to go shopping for their schoolbooks and supplies. Abis Mall was a one stop shopping Mecca for wizarding needs of every kind, and carefully hidden from the eyes of muddles. There were shops for cauldrons, wands, potions and rare potion ingredients, books, specialty foods, magical items, goats and other familiars, laboratory equipment, robes, cellphones, holy grails, astrological charts and tools, and lawnmowers. There were also shops that provided wizarding services such as spells, restaurants, banking, cleaning, tailoring, real estate, lawn mower repair, and travel. Harry had gone here every year to get his school supplies, including his most important purchase, his magic wand, for a wizard is nothing without his magic wand.

Harry had his Uncle Vermin drive him to Berlin, which was no problem, Uncle Vermin had long since come to understand the New House Order. Harry got out of the car, and went into a seemingly abandoned amusement park. It had formerly been the ill-fated experiment, Disneyland Germany. It was in a permanent state of rust. Harry jumped into a construction debris chute. The chute deposited him inside a building that looked like an abandoned warehouse from the outside. He landed in the trash dumpster, in

Abis Mall, behind The Magic Ice Shop, where wizards go to get frozen in their favorite Magic Ice flavor. He was happy that he didn't get hurt, but upset at how filthy he was, covered in sticky melted ice goo, used napkins, and bugs. Ugggh, the stink was appalling. He waved his wand and spoke the magic phrase, "AAA Dry Cleaners are the best!" (Sorry about that, folks, but product placement pays the bills, you know!) He was instantly clean, fresh, and lemon-scented.

He was a bit early so he bought a Magic Ice cone and though it was comfortable indoors, he put on the winter parka needed to eat one. He took a seat outside the shop at a table with an umbrella and waited for his friends to arrive. He glanced at the ceiling, it depicted what it was like outside, a sunny day. The illusion was perfect, he almost felt like he was outside.

As he waited for Ron and Hermione to arrive, he thought about how he would be seeing them off at the Hogwashes Express in just two days. Which reminded him of the time he first met Ron and Hermione. He met Ron at Victoria Station while looking for the right platform, Platform π (Pi), on his first day of school. That was nearly seven years ago, if you counted preschool. Harry wondered, if you don't count preschool, do you count the people you met in preschool? He gave up trying to figure that one out, as he wasn't much on philosophy, and since he did count preschool anyway.

Harry had arrived at Victoria Station alone except for his new baby goat, Headbutt, and was very nervous about how to find Platform π. He was between platforms three and four, just like Hasbeen had told him, but there was no sign of Platform π.

The wizarding community was clever in the ways it kept itself hidden from the eyes of muddles. The engineers couldn't just protect the entrance to Platform π with an illusionary wall, or some muddle might come along, and accidentally lean against the wall, only to find out there really wasn't one. They crafted the entrance to Platform π so that you had to concentrate on something rather specific and unlikely, in order to pass through the illusion, thus preventing the entrance from being discovered accidentally.

As it was, only one muddle had ever found Platform π, Lewis Carroll. That was back in 1862 when Victoria Station was known as the London, Brighton, and South Coast Railway or LBSCR. (Back then the wizards only used the first two decimal places to protect the entrance of Platform π. They immediately changed it to ten decimal places, and no muddle has found it since.) Lewis Carroll consequently gave up his career in mathematics, and wrote about his adventures in the strange world he uncovered. The muddles never believed him when he told them about it. That's why he created Alice to tell his stories, and called them fiction.

Harry was nervous and decided to ask for directions how to get to Platform π. The conductor he asked, gave him one of those looks that said, don't bother me with your stupid jokes, kid, and what's with the kid, kid? That was when he very fortunately came across the entire Cheesley family. He intuitively knew right away, that there was something special about this large strange group in Victoria Station. They looked like the kind that wouldn't be heading to Liverpool, Paris, or some other normal destination. They, like Harry, were carrying an assortment of strange affects, wearing robes, and were accompanied by an entourage of strange animals, including a small herd of goats, a rat, a vulture, a goldfish, two chickens, a pig, an orangutan, and a seal pup. The whole family had nuclear orange hair that reminded Harry of the edible orange rind of Muenster cheese. The Cheesleys were special, Harry could tell right away.

There were a half dozen Cheesleys, young and old, there to see the school-aged Cheesleys; Bill, Marsha, Jan, Cindy, Perky, Fred, George, and Ron off to school. Ron, like Harry, was starting preschool. Mrs. Cheesley instantly became the mom Harry never knew. She made him feel a lot better about his first time getting onto the elusive Platform π.

Harry remembered Mrs. Cheesley saying, "It's as easy as pi (pie?), just divide twenty-two by seven in your head down to the tenth decimal, while you run directly into that solid looking brick wall. And try not to think about what will happen if you make a math mistake."

After Harry had tried really hard and failed, he remembered how she had reassured him, "Don't worry about it, Luv, almost all new students take a couple of tries to get it right, and its not uncommon at all to see them with their broken noses and black eyes on the first day! They are sooo cute!" Harry made it on his next try. Ron of course made it on his first try, but he wasn't nearly as nervous as Harry.

Harry and Ron took their seats together in the same train compartment, that's where they first met Hermione. Sometime after the Hogwashes Express had left the station, she burst into their compartment, and asked, "You haven't seen a frog anywhere, have you? A kid named Neville Largebottom is missing his. By the way, I'm Hermione Stranger."

Ron had replied, "Oh, oh, I'm not allowed to talk to strangers!" He immediately refused to talk to Hermione, and wouldn't talk to her for half the school year. Only after he asked his mother, and got permission, did he finally start to talk to Hermione. By that time, he had a serious and well-deserved reputation for being the ultimate momma's boy.

Harry's reverie was broken as a foreign-looking man wearing a turban walked by his table muttering something that sounded like, "Cheating scumweasel!" Harry wondered what that guy's problem was. Then a lady wearing a black robe went by and he distinctly heard her say, "Drop dead, Quibbage cheater!" She was looking at him.

Harry could only stammer, "But, . . . But …"

Suddenly, two ninjas and their pet cat burst out of the windows of a nearby shop, Cutbait's Curiosities, with a crash and tinkling of broken glass. The cat hissed at Harry. One ninja was twirling nunchucks, the other drawing knives. Both had on loose black robes and masks, so that only their eyes could be seen, yet Harry had an eerie feeling that he somehow knew who it was confronting him. But who could they be? Harry didn't have time to think about it, he started fumbling with the Velcro and zipper that held his winter parka closed. He had to get to his wand quick, or in a moment, he would be dead.

However, in a moment, Harry couldn't stop laughing. The ninja with the nunchucks accidentally whacked himself in the head with his own weapon. He fell to the ground holding his head and writhing in pain. The other ninja hesitated asking, "Ron, are you ok?"

The voice further confirmed his suspicion, Harry asked, "Hermione, is that you?"

Her eyes widened. "Uh, no," she replied in a much deeper voice than before. "Die Quibbage Cheater!"

"Stop Hermione! I can explain!" And he did.

A few minutes later Harry and Hermione were helping Ron into a chair and putting Magic Ice on the lump on his head. The purple ice clashed horribly with his standard Cheesley nuclear orange hair, which was always a mess. Ron was a chunky kid with freckles. His voice tended to crack frequently, and he had grown at least an inch since Harry had seen him just three months ago. Ron was quite spastic and often tripped over his own big feet. He was clearly at that awkward teenage phase.

Hermione had a disproportionately large head. The expanse of naturally wavy strawberry-blonde hair, which she wore down to her shoulders, made her head seem even larger. She had bushy eyebrows and a noticeable mustache. Harry wondered if it would tickle if he were to …

Hermione interrupted his thoughts, asking, "So Harry, what are you going to do when you get to school? How will you keep everyone from killing you?"

"Actually, I've decided something, and I'm afraid you're not going to like it," said Harry nervously. "I've, decided that I'm not going to school this year."

He fully expected Hermione to go off on him. In the momentary silence that followed, he could hear her in his head, "Harry Putter! That's the stupidest thing I've ever heard you say!" Here it comes, he winced.

"Cool! That's very practical of you Harry, just what I'd do," she smiled.

Ron laughed, "I must have hit my head harder than I thought. I thought you just said you weren't going to school this year, and Hermione say that was for the best!"

"You heard right," replied Harry smiling too.

"But you have to go to school! You'll be a year behind us if you don't!" Ron argued automatically. He was a true friend and would miss Harry all year. Far worse, if Harry stayed behind, they would never have classes together again. Ron realized all this instantly, and his argument was entirely based on his emotions.

"I'll be dead, if I do! I'm better off alive at home, than dead at school, right?" replied Harry.

"But … But…" Ron felt Harry was wrong, but didn't know what to say.

They visited several of their favorite stores. At Til Eulenspiegel's Merry Prank Shop, Harry complained that he wished he'd be able to visit Fred and George's Magical Joke Shop in Hogsbreath. Unfortunately, he wouldn't be able to join the fun of the Hogsbreath visits, since he wasn't going to school. Hogsbreath was the wizarding community closest to Hogwashes. Students of Hogwashes generally enjoyed a weekend trip to Hogsbreath several times each year. There were several shops in Hogsbreath that students typically frequented on these trips. Fred and George Cheesley had dropped out of school last year in order to set up Fred and George's Magical Joke Shop in Hogsbreath, in the hopes that it would become a favorite of the students. Hermione pointed out that Harry was being ridiculous, he could certainly meet them at Hogsbreath for a visit. What else did he have to do? This put a ray of hope into all their hearts. It was instantly settled, Harry would meet them on their first weekend trip to Hogsbreath. That however, didn't keep Harry from spending all the money he would have used to buy schoolbooks for the upcoming year on all kinds of wicked joke items from Fred and George's only competitors. He bought a year's supply of dungbombs, silly string, farting underpants, ultra-burp soda, butt-enlarging crackers, fake wands, a dribble goblet of fire, ventrilo-whoopy cushions, glue-gum, and mace-squirting flowers.

They decided to head to the bookstore next. As Ron glanced over his list, Harry suddenly realized that he hadn't received a booklist from school.

"Hey! I never got mine," he said as he grabbed the booklist from Ron. "I never got a list from Hogwashes! What does that mean? Do they know I'm not coming to school?"

"Harry," Hermione asked, "didn't you say, that you had received an official notice that school was canceled?"

"Yeah. It had the Hogwashes seal and everything."

"Yes, but I didn't receive one. Did you Ron?"

"uhnt-uh," grunted Ron.

"You see what that means, don't you?" asked Hermione.

"That school is only canceled for Harry?" asked Ron.

"No. It means there is someone at Hogwashes that is intercepting Harry's mail. They replaced his schoolbook list with the fake cancellation notice, before it was sealed shut. It means we need to watch what we say when we write to Harry, and Harry has to be careful what he says when he writes to us."

"That means the conspiracy is real!" concluded Ron. "Crap! That means Harry shouldn't go to school. He'll be killed."

"Ron, I already explained that I'm not going to school," said Harry with exasperation.

"But I thought you were just making the whole thing up, you know, to get out of going to school," said Ron.

At Pigbristle's Quill and Bookstore, Hermione held the door open for Ron and Harry. Harry suddenly saw the gleaming smile and wavy blonde hair of their old Defense Against the Fine Arts teacher, Gildersneeze Farthard, autographing his latest book. Harry instinctively ducked behind a bookshelf, pulling Ron with him so that Farthard wouldn't see them.

Harry couldn't believe it. Gildersneeze Farthard was out of St. Mongo's Hospital for the magically afflicted. He wondered if Farthard had gotten his memory back. Farthard had a large portion of his memory wiped out during Harry's third year of school. What no one knew was that Harry and Ron were the cause. They had discovered the secret to Farthard's success. For everyone knew Farthard as a heroic adventurer. However, no one knew that Farthard was in fact stealing other people's incredible adventures for years, and was really a coward at heart. He would interview heroic individuals, wipe their memories from them, then write books about their fantastic deeds, claiming them as his own. He had become quite a celebrity in doing so. Many people referred to him as the Great Gildersneeze. It turned out that, the Great Gildersneeze was quite jealous of Harry Putter's rapidly growing popularity stemming from the boy's exciting adventures. So Farthard tried to horn in on Harry's adventures for himself. Farthard had revealed his dirty little secret and was about to wipe Harry's memory clean, when Ron, crept up on Gildersneeze, whacked him on the back of the head with a half gallon of ice cream from the Chamber of Frozen Dairy Desserts. It's not clear whether it was the blow from Ron or Farthard's subsequent knock to the head as he collapsed to the floor that ironically caused Farthard's persistent case of amnesia, his drooling problem, and the thick lisp when he spoke.

Hermione cheerfully skipped up to her old teacher and sang out, "Mr. Farthart! It's so good to see you again!"

Harry groaned and hit his head against the bookshelf several times. He thought, "How could someone so smart be so stupid!"

Farthard's smile seemed to brighten, if that was possible, he was obviously feeling loved by another fan. "You theem vaguely familiar, child, do I know you?" he asked while wiping his lip.

Hermione ignored the speckle that touched her face as Farthard spoke. "It's me! Hermione Stranger. I was one of your students at Hogwashes three years ago! Remember?" she asked.

"Well, if you are a thtranger, then I guesth I'm mithtaken, but it'th alwayth nithe to meet a fan. Would you like an autograph?" replied Gildesneeze, flourishing his pen, ready to sign another book.

Hermione disgusted, took a step back as he spoke, to avoid the shower of spittle coming from his direction. She suddenly realized that Gildersneeze probably still didn't remember much of that year at all. Of course he wouldn't remember her. She handed him a copy of his latest book, "The Ecstasy of Man-made Explosions vs. the Calamity of Natural Disaster," then retreated a step.

"Who thhould I make this out to?" he asked.

"Hermione Stranger," she replied, hiding her displeasure.

"To a mythteriouth thtranger ..." he wrote as he said aloud, "Fond wistheth ... in all your egthplothive endeavorth ... Thintherely ... Gilderthneethe Farthard!" He finished his signature with a flourish.

Hermione tried to suppress her gag reflex. She managed to just look dumbstruck.

"Thay, ith that your required reading litht from Hogwathheth?" he asked with an appauling splatter of drool.

"Yes, your latest book is on it. That's why I'm buying it," she replied in disgust.

"Well then, you'll be pleathed to know that I'll be at Hogwathheth again thith year. I'll be teaching, Defenthe againtht the Fine Artth. I believe that one'th required for all thtudentth, tho I'll thee you in clasth!" he beamed.

Harry and Ron eavesdropping from behind the bookshelf, looked at each other and screamed. Hermione shrieked.

Gildersneeze drooled, "Do try to contain yourthelf, thweet girl."

Chapter 4

Platform π (Pi)

Harry woke up early and dressed. It was the first day of school, and Harry was going to see his friends off at the train station. He went downstairs, and was glad to see all the Dirtleys were already awake. They were obviously quite used to the New House Order. Uncle Vermin was getting ready to drive him to London. He had informed Uncle Vermin the day before of his intention to see his friends off at Victoria Station. Aunt Hachooie was there to make breakfast for the family. Dudley was shining his shoes as instructed. Harry was very pleased. He had Aunt Hachooie make him his favorite breakfast, a huge ice cream sundae.

It, the ice cream sundae that is, started talking to Harry, "What a Delicious Morning! Don't I look tasty? But, brother, is it hot out here. If I stay out here, I'm gonna melt for sure."

No, Harry wasn't crazy. He was a morsel-tongue, he could hear what his food was saying, and if he chose to, he could reply. It was his special talent, mysteriously conferred upon him from Moldyfart the first time they met. As Moldyfart's powers vanished, somehow this power, the ability to talk to food, was transferred to Harry. Harry wished that he had gotten a real superpower like the ability to fly, use x-ray vision, climb on walls, or perform feats of super strength. Cripes, why couldn't he be more like Spiderman? However, talking to food was better than nothing. It did have its advantages, too, he supposed, especially if you could tell when your food was lying to you. Usually food didn't know much that would be useful, but occasionally it would overhear some gossip or other information of value.

Harry was quite used to his food talking. It no longer bothered him to eat something mid-sentence, like it used to. He found most prepared foods actually wanted you to eat them, and were more likely to tell the truth. More wholesome foods tended to beg you not to eat them, and would make up all sorts of lies to escape being severed, masticated, and decomposed by stomach acid. Food that had gone bad, always told you that they were still fresh, making it very difficult in some cases to tell the difference, until he got the knack for it.

The ice cream sundae was in a hurry to be eaten. It was entirely prepared for consumption. Harry was equally prepared to accommodate it.

When he was finished breakfast, he held his tummy and sighed happily. "Cripes! I'm getting fat!" he thought.

He relaxed for a moment, recalling the faces of all the Dirtleys when he informed them that he wasn't going to school this year. "What a classic!" he laughed to himself. Their jaws were agape with looks as dumbfounded as a bunch of Republican politicians caught in a sting operation. Since then, all he got were looks of seething and loathing. The Dirtleys hated him now. They hadn't cared for him at all before the New House Order. After, they had put up with a lot of abuse from Harry, bearing all their suffering in great dislike, looking forward to him going back to school and life becoming normal for the rest of the year. His new plan had brought that idea crashing down on their heads. Now they would have to put up with this miserable New House Order forever, or at least until someone died.

Harry suddenly wondered if he was in any danger from them. They wouldn't try to do anything to him would they? He started to worry about poison in his ice cream sundae. The sundae would have warned him if it had been poisoned, wouldn't it have? Aunt Hachooie wouldn't! Would she? She was removing a pie from the oven, but her sidelong look in his direction, made the hair on the back of his neck stand on end. He suddenly was feeling sick to his stomach. He ran to the bathroom toilet and threw up.

A few minutes later, he was feeling a bit better, and it was time to go. "Uncle Vermin, go start the car, I'll be right out." yelled Harry from the bathroom. He brushed his teeth, and then ran out to the waiting mini Cooper.

At the train station Harry got out of the car saying, "I'll be back in fifteen, twenty minutes, can you get me a hotdog and a slurpie in the meantime?" Then he added, "Please?" His stomach was obviously feeling better, and he felt benevolent by asking politely.

Harry followed a baggage cart to the entrance of Platform π where he saw several students milling about trying quickly to divide twenty-two by seven, or to just remember the first ten decimal places of π, or holding their heads after slamming them into the brick wall between platform three and four. There were also several younger ones holding their noses and wailing to their mothers. Adding to the confusion were enough goats to fill a barnyard as well as other pets, familiars, and elven servants. On top of that, there was a virtual train of baggage carts. It's easy to see why the muddles would avoid that freak show.

Harry wound his way through the chaos. Not having even the most rudimentary knowledge of mathematics, (Hogwashes doesn't teach any muddle subjects.) he was nonetheless able to attain the elusive platform on his first try. He had the first ten decimal places of π memorized. Little did he realize he was being followed.

Platform π, if anything, was even crazier than the scene outside. The Hogwashes Express looked like a circus train with two whole cars filled with goats and a third with a menagerie of other animals. Baggage was being loaded into baggage cars. Families were saying their last goodbyes. One baggage cart had been upset, and two men were arguing about it.

From a distance, Harry spotted the Cheesley family's nuclear orange hair and headed that direction, to say hello to all the Cheesleys. Bill, Greg, Marsha, Jan, Cindy, the twins, Fred and George, their mother, Molly, and their father, Arthur were all there to see Ron, Ginny, and little Suzanne off to school. Perky Cheesley was notably absent. Ron was holding a gigantic squid, with tentacles wrapped around him. "Hi Ron! What's that for?" asked Harry.

"It's my new pet! I've been raising it all summer, isn't he cute!"

Harry made a wry face and said, "Yeah, cuddly."

The way the squid wrapped its slimy tentacles around Ron's arms and neck, somehow reminded Harry of the brain-thing in the tank at the circus that had wrapped itself around Ron last spring. Harry wondered if Ron would ever be the same. Harry let the thought go.

Arthur Cheesley was saying, "Sorry to hear about the conspiracy to kill you, Harry. You're doing the right thing staying home where you'll be safe."

"That's right! I think it will be safer for everyone this way," replied Harry, trying to sound like he was doing the noble thing. Marsha, Jan, and Cindy all sighed lovingly at his words and selfless sacrifice. Harry was their hero.

"Well, it's about time you stopped endangering the other children," scolded Mrs. Cheesley. She was still upset about the constant danger Harry kept putting her school aged children in, especially Ginny. She had long ago concluded that Ron would never amount to much. Thank God that her baby, Suzanne, wouldn't be around him as she started preschool this year.

He was warmly greeted by all the other Cheesleys especially Ginny, who cried out, "I'm going to miss you Harry Putter!" She jumped up wrapping her arms and legs around Harry and smothered him with kisses until her father pulled her off from Harry disapprovingly.

Little Suzanne stomped on Harry's foot, and gave him a raspberry. It was her way of showing him, how much she, too, liked him. It was her first year at Hogwashes, but she didn't seem nervous at all.

Just then Hermione called from the train, "Hurry up girls, the train leaves in ten minutes! I saved you a seat Ron!" Ron blushed, embarrassed to know her. "Harry!" she shouted, "I didn't think you were going to make it."

Harry glanced at the clock, there was indeed still ten minutes before the train departed. "Are you kidding, Hermione, I wouldn't miss this if Lord Moldyfart had me chained up in a dungeon somewhere."

The crowd immediately went quiet, even the goats became silent. For seldom was the name Moldyfart spoken in public, and when it was it was usually at a whisper at best. Most chose to refer to him as the Fart Lord, "He-Who-Must-Not-Be-Smelled," Mr. Stinky, or Lord Pull-My-Finger. However, Harry didn't seem to care about the disapproving looks coming from all directions. By contrast, Ron took out a paper bag, and pulled it over his own head, wishing that he had gotten on the train already.

"In fact," Harry continued loudly, "I wish Lord Moldyfart had tried to keep me away!"

The crowd started to murmur at this. There were a few angry shouts. "Shut up you, twit!" and "It's that cheating git, Putter! Kill him."

Ron whispered to Harry, "Ix nay on the Oldyfart May."

George and Fred Cheesley were enjoying the scene immensely. If Ron was embarrassed, they were all for it. They had themselves created quite a public spectacle when they suddenly dropped out of school last year in history-making fashion.

"How's it going Harry?" asked Fred. "Haven't seen you in months, you've got to stop by the joke shop sometime. I want you to try out our newest feature, anti-matter toothpaste. It's hilarious!"

"Sounds great," Harry replied, "I've been meaning to visit the shop one of these days." He felt a twinge of guilt for having bought all that stuff at their competitor's joke shop. "How's the store doing?"

"Not bad, we've held our own, and should start turning a profit with the return of the students."

Just then, Looney Luvnoodle and Neville Largebottom arrived. Neville was a pear shaped lump of a young man, who was very forgetful, a marginal student, and suffered from chronic asthma. By contrast, Looney was a large and athletic young woman, a sharp student, and very open-minded. Her father was the owner of *The Dribbler*, a wizardly world tabloid that most regarded as the least newsworthy of all tabloids, considering it to be entirely fiction. Harry noticed they were holding hands as they approached him.

"Hello, Harry," said Neville.

"Hi Harry," said Looney.

Neville Largebottom and Looney Luvnoodle were both instrumental in helping Harry last spring. Harry had been tricked. The Fungus Eaters had set him up. They leaked information to Harry of the whereabouts of his uncle, Serious Smack the Clown. Harry couldn't help fall into their trap, finding his uncle was his vulnerability, and they took full advantage of it, setting a trap for when Harry arrived at the circus. If it weren't for friends like Neville and Looney, that helped him that day, he himself might not have survived. As it turned out, his uncle wasn't so fortunate.

Harry choked as the raw emotions of that day hit him suddenly with the entrance of Neville and Looney. He hadn't seen them since. Everything seemed to remind him of his lost uncle.

Harry tried to compose himself, as Neville and Looney told him the good news. "We've been seeing each other all summer," Neville announced.

Harry congratulated them with a burst of tears, and wished them well during the upcoming school year.

Something in his tone alerted Looney, she replied, "You sound as though you're not going?"

"I'm not," Harry sobbed. He composed himself, then explained the whole reason why he wasn't.

The train whistle blew and the conductor called out for all passengers to board, it was time to say goodbye. Harry shook Ron's hand and said, "Don't forget to send me a goat every so often, to tell me how school's going!"

"Don't forget to send me a goat every so often, to tell me how your extended summer vacation is going," laughed Ron.

The Cheesleys all wished Ron, Ginny, and Suzanne good luck in school, and gave them hugs and kisses. A few minutes later, they were aboard, along with their baggage. Then the Cheesley family turned to Harry and said their goodbyes. They all wished him a good year off from school.

"I wish I could stay home from school too, you lucky dog!" said Hermione from her train compartment window. "Imagine how much I would learn then!" It was true, Hermione hadn't learned anything at school the last two years, and had calculated her education to be three full years ahead of the rest of her class. She was already teaching herself post-graduate wizarding studies. She typically spent the summer educating herself, and the school year educating others.

Mrs. Cheesley asked Harry, "Do you have a ride home?"

"Yes," he replied, "Uncle Vermin is waiting for me out in the car."

"A car!" Arthur and Molly Cheesley laughed at the muddle idea of driving. Then most of the Cheesleys grabbed hold of their bottle of port and instantly teleported to the Boil, that's what they called their home. Fred and George were the only Cheesleys with enough magic power to teleport without a portal key, or as those who could teleport called it, abbarate. They hastily said goodbye, worried that Harry might hit them up for some of the money they owed him. "See ya, soon." They abbarated back to their shop, leaving Harry standing alone.

A moment later, as Harry turned the corner to walk up the platform stairs, a damp cloth suddenly clamped over his nose and mouth, while strong hands seized him roughly. He felt his legs collapse under him and his last sight before blacking out was of Uncle Vermin, Aunt Hachooie, and Mudley Dirtley giving each other high fives. Uncle Vermin held a rag and a bottle in his hand. Mudley had an enormous suitcase, and Aunt Hachooie was holding a slice of pie. "I thought he was on to me! Who bakes a pie at six in the morning?" laughed Aunt Hachooie.

Harry's last thought was, "π.....pi....pie! How ingenious!"

Chapter 5

On the Hogwashes Express

During the long trip to Hogwashes, Ron, Ginny, Suzanne, and Hermione shared a train compartment. Ron knew instinctively the situation was all wrong. It was against the unwritten code for a teenage boy to hang out with girls, especially sisters. Hermione's cat, Croakshanks, was nestled in her lap. Ron's pet squid, Nemoy, was squirming its ten tentacles around Ron. As students passed by their compartment, they glanced in through the window, and were obviously excited about their discovery. Ron's ears were ringing. He knew that he was going to hear comments later, and was getting in a bad mood just anticipating the ribbing he would have to face.

The truth was, Hermione and he were friends, but the bigger truth was that they were both friends of Harry's. Could they remain friends without Harry? He knew that others would start calling Hermione his girlfriend, probably later that day. That would be embarrassing; Hermione was as big a nerd as they came. She had to hang out with Harry and Ron because the girls wouldn't accept her into their fold, not even the other girl Nerds. What's worse, how would he ever find a girlfriend, if she were around? Ron felt very self aware now that the fragile dynamic was broken. He wondered if there were any other Nerds he could hang out with, and if he started to hang out with other Nerds, would Hermione's feeling be hurt? Of course they would. He couldn't do that to her, she'd have no friends. His mood worsened as he thought about his predicament. It made him unconsciously argumentative, and he wasn't in a place where he could win arguments. Furthermore, losing argument after argument only worsened his mood, making him snappish.

Ron and Hermione argued about anything and everything. Ron argued from the pit of his belly, entirely based on his feelings. Hermione's arguments were irrefutably based on logic. Ginny stuck a barb into Ron whenever the opportunity presented itself. Suzanne usually just laughed or inserted her own silly comments, which were mostly ignored.

Ron tried talking about subjective topics, to avoid losing, for everyone is entitled to their opinion. However, Hermione was able to show him that his opinion was usually wrong.

They argued about their duties as Perfects. The Perfects were the Hogwashes hall monitors. Their job was to keep the other kids from running in the hall, fighting in the hall, smoking in the halls, kissing in the halls, or starting food fights in the Great Eatery. That last one was added after the huge food fight in the Great Eatery last year. Most of the other kids referred to the Perfects as either Mr. Perfect or Ms. Perfect according to gender. Ron and Hermione were both Perfects, and did their best to set a good example to the other students, by not breaking any of the rules. Harry, of course, could never be a Perfect; he broke all the rules. Ron and Hermione could have written him up for hundreds of incidents, but never did.

They argued about Free-Elves. Hermione had long held the opinion that Free-Elves sapped a small amount of power from their masters, and provided very little in return, especially if one was to take excellent care of their own magical equipment, which she always did. Elves were her pet peeve, especially since she was always being bothered by elves who wanted to serve her. (She had excellent magical powers.) Some elves even pretended to be in danger. They would try to trick her into "saving" their lives, thereby hoping to force their unwanted service upon her. She seemed very callous at times when an elf would be for example "drowning" in the nearby Jello, and she wouldn't even lift a spoon to save them. Ron always felt bad for them, and tried to save them, which would make them snap and growl at him, or abberate in order to avoid him all together.

She also felt that using Elves was wrong whether they were Free-Elves or not. She felt that it would be better to pay elves for their services, if one really desired them. Three years ago, she formed the OSPREE Club, also known as the Only Stupid People Rely on Elven Exploitation Club. Even Harry and Ron didn't join that one, and they didn't even have elven servants. Heck, even the elves wouldn't join; they snubbed their noses at the idea of their noble service being paid for in coin. In reality, she would have been far happier if she just accepted a Free-Elf's service. If she did, no other Elves would bother her, and she wouldn't even notice the small difference in her magical powers.

They especially argued about Harry not coming to school. Ron couldn't get past how much he was going to miss Harry. With Harry, school was always exciting. Being friends with Harry, who was always in the spotlight, Ron got to share a little bit of the spotlight, too. He felt special. He thought aloud, "It's like you, me, and Harry were a shiny new tricycle! Each of us one wheel."

Hermione replied, "Well, think of us as a bicycle now! A bicycle is much smarter than a tricycle! It's more grown up. School is going to be great this year, think of all you will learn, especially without all the distractions that Harry always made. I'll bet your grades will go up considerably this year."

Ron disagreed, "But it's not like a bicycle, it's like a tricycle without one wheel. We'll be missing an important part of what made us a great team. You were like the brains, I was the good-looking one, and Harry was …errr, …dynamic, you know? He was like the big wheel with the pedals on it. He made it all work."

Ginny and Suzanne started laughing, and couldn't stop. Suzanne didn't even know why she was laughing, other than the fact that Ginny was laughing at Ron, so she should too. It was a principle between brothers and sisters.

Ginny imitated her brother, "Look at me, I'm the good looking one!" Suzanne giggled. Ron ignored them.

Hermione bit her tongue, "Well, I think we can still be a great team, I'm still smart and you're ….ummm….not any different. We don't need Harry to have a great year at Hogwashes. Learning is exciting enough without adding his dramatics, –OOH, look at me, the Fart Lord is after me, he wants to kill me."

Hermione was getting annoyed with Ron; he was so immature at times. Just look at the immature garbage he had bought when the refreshment cart had come by. Chocolate slugs, Yu-Gi-Oh! cards, and Every-Witch-Way beans. It was the same crap he bought the past five years, six if you counted preschool. He had already stuffed five of the chocolate slugs in his face. Two, ok, but five? Gross. Sometimes she wished he would grow up. He didn't seem the least bit interested in girls.

Likewise, Ron was annoyed. Hermione was practically talking badly about Harry. Some fan she was! He decided to lead her down a different path. "Well, what I really think is that his staying home is really just a cry for…"

Just then they both turned to the door. From outside their compartment, they heard a tiny, distant, and muffled cry, "Help, Help!"

Hermione replied, "Nonsense, Harry will be safest at home. And from what he said, he's had the best summer of his life."

Ron retorted, "Being home, isn't like being on 'base' in a game of tag. He might be in just as much danger there, possibly more since we won't be there to…"

"Help, Help!" the muffled cry got a little louder, causing Ron to look at the window in the train compartment door. Hermione,

Ginny, and Suzanne all followed his gaze. The cry for help was getting even louder, and then Faco Maldoy crossed their window view. He was heading toward the back of the train. He appeared to be dragging something rather heavy, walking backwards as he dragged it.

Faco Maldoy was the son of Luscious Maldoy, the same Luscious Maldoy who was Chairman of the Board of Education at Hogwashes, the same Luscious Maldoy who lost his Free-Elf servant Bobby, thanks to Harry. What's more, Luscious Maldoy was one of the Fungus Eaters. The Fungus Eaters were a group of evil supporters of Lord Moldyfart, and Luscious Maldoy was one of their highest-ranking members. He was the one who had conceived the plot to lure Harry to the circus where his uncle was, in order to trap him, and turn him over to Lord Moldyfart. His involvement in setting the trap last spring had compromised him. Finally, the Harry Putter Fan Club had the evidence they needed that Luscious was indeed a Fungus Eater, as they all had long suspected. More importantly, the Ministry of Magic authorities had the evidence they needed to prosecute Maldoy and the other Fungus Eaters for the murder of Serious Smack the Clown. Consequently, Luscious Maldoy, as well as a number of other identified Fungus Eaters, were on the run from the Ministry of Magic, and in hiding. They of course blamed their situation on Harry Putter.

Faco Maldoy was of course a Popular Rich Kid. He was tall, handsome, with an athletic body, and blonde down to his brain. Faco was in the same year of school as Harry, Ron, and Hermione, and in many of their classes. He was also a Perfect, which gave him a smug satisfaction. He was one, while Harry was not.

Harry and Faco had clashed ever since their second day of preschool, six years ago. It was "show and tell" day. While all the other kids brought in their favorite, cool, and in some cases very expensive toys, Harry had brought in his dust-bunny collection.

Hermione remembered Faco's derisive words to this day, "What's the matter with you Putter? Don't you have any real toys?" She quietly kept her mold collection in her backpack, and said she had forgotten her "show and tell."

Since then, Faco was a constant adversary of theirs, although their spats with him were minor when compared to the life and death struggles they had so far with his father and Lord Moldyfart.

If Faco had any secret contact with his father since last spring, he was likely to know about all of the students who helped Harry defeat Faco's father and the rest of the Fungus Eaters. He would most likely attempt to exact some form of retribution as revenge on Ron, Hermione, Neville, Looney, and Ginny. He also wouldn't be alone in his efforts. He often consorted with two brainless but muscular goons, Shabby and Foil, each of whose fathers were Fungus Eaters and likewise on the run from Ministry authorities.

"Oh, no, it's Maldoy!" said Ron. He was suddenly nervous; his proximity to Harry had long been the source of his safety from Maldoy and his bullies. What was he going to do without Harry around this year to protect him? He'd have to avoid confronting Faco for as long as possible, and hope that the bullies would bother someone else.

"Help, Help!" called the muffled voice.

"For Pete's sake! Give him a hand with the door, Ron!" said Hermione.

"I don't see why I should, except that I won't have to look at him as long," said Ron, getting up, trying to sound like he wasn't intimidated, and failing miserably as his voice cracked.

"Here, hold this," Ron held Nemoy out to Hermione.

"No! NO! I mean it Ron, get that thing away from me."

Ron sighed, went into the hallway, and held open the door for Faco as he wheeled a humongous suitcase onto the next train car. He wondered why Faco was moving his own luggage; usually the

Popular Rich Kids had servants to move their luggage for them. Thank God, Shabby and Foil weren't around.

Faco glanced at Ron and did a double take. "Ewwwww, what's that thing?"

"Huh? Oh, you mean Nemoy? He's my pet squid," replied Ron.

"Cheesley you are one sick freak. You better not get any of that slime on me if you know what's good for you."

"Help, Help!" came the muffled cry from the suitcase.

"I don't think that should be too hard."

"I'll have Shabby and Foil rearrange your face. When they get through with you, no one will know the difference between you and that ugly octopus."

"Yeah, nice to see you again too, Faco. You haven't lost any of your charm, I see."

"Shut your mouth, slimeball."

"Shut yours, ..." Ron's retort was cut short when one of Nemoy's tentacles suddenly curled into his mouth. Ron let go of the door to remove it. Faco was repulsed.

"Uuuuuck," said Ron, wiping his tongue off on the sleeve of his robe.

Ron returned to his compartment saying, "Furthermore, ... wait a sec, was that Harry's voice coming from that suitcase?"

"Harry, here? We left him back at the station," Hermione sniffed.

"Hermione, come quick!" shouted Ron dashing out of the compartment. Hermione was right behind him. Ginny and Suzanne in tow.

They ran through the train cars and quickly caught up to Faco moving his large burden. "All right, Maldoy, open the suitcase!" commanded Ron, trying to sound confident.

Faco looked up at Cheesley and his entourage, "Still hanging out with the other girls, Cheesley?"

"I mean it, open that suitcase, now!"

"Get lost, Cheesley, mind your own business," replied Maldoy sounding a lot more commanding than Ron.

"Cripes, Ron, is that you?" came the muffled voice of Harry from inside the suitcase.

"Oh my God, it is Harry!" said a shocked Hermione.

"Hand it over, Maldoy!" shouted Ron.

"I said, get lost, Cheesley!" Faco shouted back.

Ron decided to go for his wand first and get the upper hand on Maldoy before Maldoy got his wand out and got the upper hand on him. "Ha HA! I've got you now, Maldoy!" he said triumphantly.

However, Maldoy was so close to Ron in the small aisle that he reached out quickly with one hand, pinched the end of Ron's wand, and twisted it firmly upward. With a snap, the tip of the wand broke and dangled from the end of Ron's wand. Ron was too slow as he said the entire magic command, "It takes a tough man to make a tender chicken." It was too late. The sudden burst of power from the broken wand caused a flash of light, and a fizzling pop.

Ron said, "No, OH! Wand my broke you."

Maldoy laughed at the gibberish, "You always were a backward sort, Cheesley." But his laughing was cut short when Hermione's knee met his groin. He collapsed to the floor and started moaning like a banshee with a hangover.

Hermione unzipped the suitcase, and a hot and sweaty Harry Putter rolled out. He was quite relieved to finally get a breath of fresh air. He stretched out his stiff legs.

"Harry, what are you doing in there?" she asked.

"?Suitcase that in get you did how" asked Ron.

Harry looked at Ron puzzled.

"The Dirtleys kidnapped me! They knocked me out, packed me in that suitcase, and put me in the baggage compartment. When I came to, I didn't know where I was. I couldn't reach my wand, so I called for help. Unfortunately, Maldoy found me first.

"All after year this school to going you're like looks," said Ron. They all laughed, but only Ron's sounded like, "Ah, Ah, Ah!"

Chapter 6

Dieters Beware!

Harry stood alone and unnoticed for a moment in the entrance to the Great Eatery. Ron had gone immediately to the hospital wing to take care of his speech impediment. Hermione had accompanied him. She explained, "Just in case Madame Pomfrite doesn't understand him when he talks."

The students were assembling in the Great Eatery, which was decked out in banners and flags for each of the four Noble Houses at Hogwashes. The ceiling showed what it was like outside, a clear evening with stars beginning to shine, which had nothing to do with the actual weather outside, nor did it predict the weather tomorrow. The ceiling had been broken for years, and was useless as it always predicted yesterday's weather. Still it did make a nice decoration, and made the Great Eatery seem even larger than it actually was.

The hall was lit by detached floating florescent light bulbs. A few of them flickered annoyingly. The lights cast a purplish hue on everyone's skin, making all look morbidly depressing. In some cases, it was difficult to tell the living from the dead, especially since the dead were among the living. Several phantoms, ghosts, full torso apparitions, washed-up television stars, zombies, mummies, and poltergeists were interspersed among those in attendance, intermixed with the students collectively sitting at four long rows of tables, one for each of the Houses.

At the tables for the Athletic Jock House, students were wearing sweatpants and jerseys and busied themselves with horseplay or were talking excitedly about sport events and statistics. Peeved the Poltergeist yanked Michael Coronary's sweatpants down to his ankles unexpectedly, revealing his green briefs for all to see. Coronary yanked them back up as he turned mottled purple, flushing. Then Harry spotted Yu Rang and his heart skipped a beat. He hadn't seen her since school let out. Even in this light, he thought she looked... well, yeah, he admitted, even she looked gruesome in this light. However, hers was a wonderful kind of gruesome that made butterflies dance in his stomach.

Meanwhile at the tables reserved for the Popular Rich Kids House students were mostly talking on cell phones, or admiring each other's taste in new designer clothes. (Cell phones were a topic of much debate among the wizarding community. The muddles had outdone them, and the wizards to their shame couldn't come up with anything that could compete with convenience, ease, and clarity of a cell phone. Hence, young wizards and witches were using cell phones everywhere these days, much to the distaste of generations of their elders.) Quite a few were catching up on the latest gossip stories from the summer. The most popular of the ghosts, the charismatic Muddy-Cruddy Baron, was telling one of his war stories to a group that had gathered around him listening fascinated. He could tell a good tale.

At the tables for The Nerd House, students looked nervous, and a few were playing practical jokes on one another. Some were busy discussing that year's Tea Cup Tournament. Others were talking about Star Trek. Many were reading. Nearly-Earless Nick was making his friendly rounds among the Nerds, asking each about their summer. He was quite jealous of the Baron because he had such great tales to tell, and told them so well. Nick competed in his own way, for he had a wonderful personality, and was an excellent conversationalist.

The Party Animal House students were just starting to come to life this early in the evening. Quite a few were obviously asleep. One could hear the fizz of Alka Seltzer from glasses in front of those who had hangovers from partying extremely hard on their last night of summer. Most of the Party Animals wore dark sunglasses hiding their eyes, the symbol of their noble house. Even their undead had adopted the habit of wearing dark sunglasses indoors. Cries of "DUDE!" rang out as Charlie Cartuffle approached them. Charlie was so cool. Everyone thought so. He was so at ease with his own popularity, which only contributed to his aura of coolness. Harry was inwardly jealous. He never felt at ease with his own popularity, he felt like a dork most of the time. Comparing Harry to Charlie was a lot like comparing Nearly Earless Nick to the Muddy Cruddy Baron.

There was one other set of tables, across the front of the room, where the teachers were gathering and chatting about their summer activities, and how short the break always was. Professor Ape, the head of the Popular Rich Kids House and Poisons class teacher, was talking with Professor Snout, who taught how to find roots and truffles in the forest, that is, The Forbidden Forest of Sure Death. Gildersneeze Farthard was there too, talking with Cubious Hasbeen, the groundskeeper and manager of the Magical Creatures Petting Zoo in the back of the school. Mrs. Tickwick and Mrs. Fatfree had their heads together whispering. The centaur, Frenzy, who taught Astro-numerology stood a hoof and aloof nearby. The teachers too were not without their undead. Professor Binge, the History of Magic teacher, had died from over-eating (his stomach exploded), yet refused to give up teaching in his non-corporeal form.

Slightly less conspicuous were the teachers that were missing. The Head of Hogwashes, Elvis Grumblesnore wasn't there yet, nor was Professor McGooglesnot, the Head of the Nerd House, nor the

School Custodian, Belch. Grumblesnore most likely was waiting to make his grand entrance. McGooglesnot would be busy readying the first year students. The absence of Belch however, probably meant he had caught someone breaking a rule already, was out patrolling the dungeons for mischief-makers, or was cleaning up vomit somewhere.

Immediately in front of the teacher's table was a stool with a big black hat on it. The Snorting Hat, which all the students were familiar with, was used on the first day of each school year. Soon Professor McGooglesnot would lead the preschool students in, and place the Snorting Hat on each of their heads. The Snorting Hat would quickly absorb the details of the most embarrassing thing that ever happened to them, and inform everyone present while make snorting sarcastic and derisive remarks. Some were fortunately quickly forgotten, while others were never to be let go. Some endured nicknames that stuck for the rest of their lives, like "Crybaby Peepants" Jones or "King Klutz" Kingly. The information was used to decide what house the person belonged in. McGooglesnot inevitably taking the students no other house would take into the Nerd House.

Suddenly, the room became quiet as the gathered crowd finally noticed Harry in the entrance. Harry saw the dagger-like stares of the entire room focused on him.

"The letters were forged! I'm not a cheater!" he yelled. The crowd booed and hissed while throwing silverware and cups at him. (Had food been served, he would have been covered with it.) He took his regular seat at the Nerds table, and kept his head down.

A sudden fanfare split the air, and Elvis Grumblesnore performed, "I'm All Shook Up" using the teacher's table as a stage. His robe and conical hat were covered with rhinestones that winked brilliantly in the spotlight. His long white beard swooped as he gyrated his hips. As he finished singing, he slid across the table on his knees to much delighted clapping, cheering, and whistling. Elvis got up off his knees and when the cheering died down said, "I have a few words to say!"

The cheers immediately rose again. Many of the girls were screaming. When it finally died back down, he drawled, "Thank you very much!" The room erupted in shrieks from the female students. One teacher fainted.

"I would like to begin by welcoming this year's new students. We will then enjoy a meal together, and at the conclusion of tonight's affair, I will go over this year's House Cup Rules. So without further adieu, lets have a warm welcome for this year's crop of new students."

Elvis led the applause as the preschool students filed in, lead by Professor McGooglesnot. She called up the first new student to be snorted, "Seymour Butz."

When all the preschool children had all been sufficiently snorted at and placed in their houses, the feast commenced. Elvis clapped his hands and food appeared on golden plates as if by magic. Everyone collectively oohed and ahhed at the scrumptious looking feast. There were blast-end toot chops and applesauce, hot fairy wings, and bogglethwart alfredo, along with many fantastic side dishes. The older children waited as the new students were all given the chance to serve themselves first. Everyone had a good laugh as the first year students tried to take the food. Their hands passed right through it. As real as it all looked, it was all an elaborate illusion; none of it was real.

After a while Elvis composed himself, wiped a tear from his eye, and stood up. "I'm sorry children, that little joke always cracks me up. At the end of the year we will hold a feast just like this, only with real food. Do not fret, you will all be fed nutritious meals until then, starting right now. Henry our head Kitchen-Elf has prepared a very nice.... ummm ...noodley meatish dish for tonight. SLOP 'EM, HENRY!"

Several Kitchen-Elves wearing empty sacks of flour or rice wheeled a huge vat out from the service entrance. It was filled with a pasty looking casserole. Henry scooped out a baseball-sized lump from the vat and splorked it into the first child's bowl, then continued quickly up and down the tables dolling out lumps of dinner to the children. A lot of kids just started eating, others without a word of complaint ignored their dish. One preschool student looked at the gray lumps of meat in their neighbor's bowl, and said, "But I'm a vegetarian!"

Henry, without looking at the child, slopped 'em a portion and said, "That's alright, it's not really meat," then moved to fill the next child's bowl. Henry didn't bother serving the Popular Rich Kid's table, as none of them ever ate the food he prepared. Nor did he serve the Party Animal's table, as they only used his meals to start food fights. There had been a terrible one last year. Those two houses subsisted almost entirely on delivery.

At last, Ron and Hermione arrived. When Hermione saw that dinner had just started, she said, "Darn, I thought we might have missed it."

Harry was one of the few who actually liked the food. It was edible, and he had subsisted on far less to eat for so long, that he quite enjoyed any food, no matter how unpalatable it was. As a matter of fact, the more unpalatable it was, the more likely there would be more for him to eat, or in some cases, more than he could eat. Friends often offered him theirs, when they just weren't hungry enough.

Nearly Earless Nick approached Harry. "Welcome back, Mr. Putter!"

"It's good to be back, Nick," Harry replied. "How have you been?"

"Most fantoobulus," said Nick, "but I hear that there is a conspiracy to kill you, young man."

At this, Harry choked. When he had recovered, he whispered, "Why, yes, I suppose there is."

"Exciting! Tell me, do you have a plan to thwart them?"

"Yes, I plan to stay alive," Harry said sarcastically.

"Brilliant!" Nick shouted. "The Muddy Cruddy Baron is taking bets that you'll snuff it by the end of this year, he's offering four to one odds. I think I'll take that wager, put a bit of lifeforce on the table, if you will. Good luck to you, Harry."

"Good luck to you, too," Harry replied. He couldn't think of a time he had said something and meant it more.

When the repast was over, Grumblesnore stood once again. "Well, thank God that stupid hat didn't try to sing a song again this year, what? What?" There was a smatter of polite applause.

"For our new students, I call your attention to this year's House Cup rules. Each year we hold a contest. The house that earns the most points wins the contest. You earn points in the following ways. Number one, by being a good student and answering questions correctly in class. Teachers will award points to the students. They can also subtract points for misbehavior in their classrooms. Two, playing quibbage. Each house's team earns points on the quibbage field, a victory in an official match will count as 25 points toward your house total. Three, by obeying the school safety rules. Our Perfects will help ensure that you do, by subtracting points from your house for misconduct in the halls. A list of all school rules is posted in each of the houses' Common Rooms. I strongly suggest you read and live them. And four, by staying out of The Forbidden Forest of Sure Death. Should any student enter The Forbidden Forest of Sure Death, not only will they surely perish, but their body will most likely be unrecoverable, and more importantly, your house will lose ten points for each member who dies without approval. Any questions?"

One newly snorted preschool girl with flaming orange hair stood up at the Party Animal table. It was little Suzanne Cheesley.

A murmur ran through the audience.

"Yes?" Grumblesnore encouraged.

"Like, what's the prize for winning?"

"Prize? Why what prize could be greater than the pride you will feel should your house win such a coveted trophy?"

"Oh, so, like, there's no prize then?"

"No," Grumblesnore chewed his lip in anger, "there is no other reward."

Suzanne sat down, and all the Party Animal's congratulated her for sticking it to the Headmaster and his stupid contest.

Grumblesnore didn't offer to answer any further questions, saying, "I'm sure you are all tired from your long journey, and classes start tomorrow morning, so be sure to get a goodnight sleep. Goodnight, y'all."

The students began exiting from the Great Eatery, only to clog the area immediately outside. Harry waited with the throngs who couldn't exit.

While he waited, Yu Rang approached him with a deep wordless groan. She towered over him, the tallest girl in the school.

"H-Hello, Yu," was all Harry could manage to say as he stared up at her, a lump in his throat.

He felt embarrassed, and impatient to leave, but something wasn't right. "Something must have happened," he thought as he waited. Everyone was craning their necks to see what was going on outside.

"So, did you have a good summer?" he bantered.

Yu Rang answered with a long groan of dismay.

Someone called for Professor McGooglesnot. She pushed her way through the congregated crowd outside the Great Eatery. Harry, Ron, and Hermione followed in her wake, much to Harry's relief. He didn't know why it was so difficult to talk to a beautiful girl like Yu.

Outside the Great Eatery was Custodian Belch. He was lying on the ground holding his stomach. Next to him was a wooden stool where a disposable pie tin rested, inside was a sole graham cracker crumb and a used fork. Immediately above him was a printed sign taped to the wall. It read:

The Chamber of Cheesecakes has been opened.
Dieter's beware!
The best Cheesecakes ever made!
Just 12 Galleys each.
Try a sample, if you dare.

Belch groaned, "OH! I can't believe I ate the whole thing! Oh! I was just going to try a bite. I read the sign. OH! 'Best cheesecake ever made' and I said to myself 'best cheesecake ever made, my foot! Grandma Belch makes the best cheesecake ever!' So, I tried it, and curse it! It's a thousand times better than me Grandmama's! Ouch! Forgive me, Grandmama! So I had some more, and then some more, and ouch, I couldn't put it down. I ate and ate until there wasn't any more left. Oh!"

Professor McGooglesnot waved her wand and said, "Wigwamia Levi-straussa!" Belch still groaning, began to levitate, hoisted up by the seat of his pants. "Ernie Mackelroy, please push Mr. Belch to the hospital wing, and tell Nurse Pomfrite what has happened."

She pushed her index finger on the moist graham cracker crumb. The morsel stuck to the end of her finger. She lifted it to her nose and sniffed. Then she placed the crumb in her mouth. A moan of dismay passed her lips.

Then Professor McGooglesnot said to the crowd, "Students, I cannot emphasize strongly enough that should any of you see a similar sign or cheesecake appearing anywhere in Hogwashes, that under no circumstances should you try it. I cannot warn you strongly enough the danger you will be in should the next cheesecake be eaten in its entirety without saving a slice for yours truly. If only I could impress upon you just how much I love cheesecake! Therefore, I am willing to give five hundred points, no make that one thousand points, to the house that brings me the next sample cheesecake!"

This announcement was followed by a huge cheer from the gathered crowd. Then, as the crowd started to disperse, it fell into many loud and excited conversations of which Harry's, Ron's, and Hermione's was just one. The students all wanted answers. What was the Chamber of Cheesecakes? Were the cheesecakes as good as Belch said? Once you started to eat one, could you stop? Or would you eat until you were laid up like Belch? Were they really worth twelve galleys each? That's quite a lot for a cheesecake! And, just who was responsible for them? Most of all, they wanted to know, where could one get one of these wonderful desserts?

Hermione, Harry, and Ron, were excitedly asking the same questions, plus a few more. Did the Chamber of Cheesecakes have anything to do with the sinister Chamber of Frozen Dairy Deserts? Was the same insane wizard, Sloberic Slipperin, responsible for this newly opened chamber, too? Would another terrible creature be guarding this chamber as well? Which was better, the steadfast classic, strawberry cheesecake, or the more modern delight, pumpkin cheesecake? While many answers eluded them, they quickly decided that with Custodian Belch incapacitated in the hospital wing, they could search after curfew, without fear of being caught outside their rooms, to see if they could find the hidden Chamber of Cheesecakes or at the very least a sample pie.

The Nerd House common room was abuzz with talk about cheesecake. Everyone wanted everyone else's opinion. Harry loudly told everyone who asked him, "I'm sure there will be plenty of opportunity for cheesecake for everyone, what I want is a good night sleep so I'm fresh for the first day of classes. He kept his real plans secret. After a short while, Ron, Hermione, and Harry excused themselves from the Nerd House Common Room early to go to bed.

Then hours after curfew, Harry woke up, slipped out from under his four-poster bed, and tipped toed over to Ron's. He pulled back the drape and was momentarily surprised to see Ron's eyes open. For a moment, he thought Ron was dead, and then Ron let out a snore. He was sleeping with his eyes open.

"Ron, you are so weird," Harry whispered as he shook his friend awake.

They each quietly constructed dummies in their beds, to make it look like someone was sleeping there, should anyone peek in past the curtains of their beds. They used a couple of extra pillows and Ron's clothes straight from his trunk.

Normally, Harry would have used his special cloak. Normally Harry would have checked his special map, the Malarky Map. However, these items were with all his other belongings back at 4 Privy Dr. But, with Belch out of the way, there was little need for caution. They simply slipped out of their room, without awakening their other two roommates, Shameonus Finnigan and Spleen Thomas.

Ron whispered, "Wait!" He crept back in to their room, and came out carrying Nemoy, his pet squid. Ron had fished the sea creature out of its special tank. Harry was puzzled as to why anyone would want to bring a giant squid along on an exploratory search. Then again, he didn't understand why Ron wanted a squid for a pet in the first place.

They met Hermione in the now empty Nerd House Common Room, and tiptoed outside as quietly as they could, so as not to disturb the stillness of the night.

Harry gently closed the portrait of the two fat ladies that hid the entrance to the Nerd House. The large women remained snoring on their canvas.

"Hello, Harry!"

"Hi Harry!"

"Holy Crap! What the heck are you two doing sneaking up on us like that?" jumped Harry.

It was Ginny Cheesley and Looney Luvnoodle.

"Sorry, didn't mean to surprise you. Getting a late start aren't you?" replied Ginny.

"Errr, late start for what?"

"Searching for the Chamber of Cheesecake, nearly everyone's been out combing the halls and dungeons for the past three hours. No one's found it yet though, not one pie. Though we did find an ancient Scottish burial tomb, and National Geographic wants to interview us tomorrow. A few others found some neat stuff, too. One of the Party Animals found a portal to Electric Underwear, you know, that exclusive American nightclub? Oh, and someone from the Athletic Jocks said he found a time machine and traveled back in time to visit Ancient Egypt, but we think he's lying."

Harry stared dumbstruck.

"Oh, well, we're beat, been up searching for hours, good luck, you three. Don't stay up too late." Ginny gave Harry a kiss full on the lips.

"Gulp, goodnight," he croaked. Ginny slipped inside the Nerd House Common Room. Looney said goodbye and headed to the Locker Room, that's what everyone called the Jock Common Room, including the Jocks.

"What was that?" asked Ron disgusted, "You got something for my little sister?"

"What? No! I ...."

"I'd better not see THAT ever happen again! Or else!" Ron shook his knuckles under Harry's nose. Harry didn't find it particularly scary, but decided it best not to upset Ron any further.

"Ron, I'm as surprised as you are. I never expected Ginny to do that!"

"What? You're blaming this on her?" Ron was starting to turn red in the face with fury.

"Ron, Ginny likes Harry, a lot, she always has! Remember how she kissed him all over his face in the train station?" said Hermione, trying to defuse the situation.

"What! Ginny would never do that! What are you talking about? She has a boyfriend, whatsisname."

"She broke up with him last year! What's the matter with you Ron? Don't you ever talk to her? It turned out she was only going out with Michael Coronary because he reminded her of Harry. She accidentally even called him Harry a few times, so he broke up with her."

"Oh," said Ron chewing his lip. "So, Harry, do you like Ginny?"

"Oh, my god, Ron! Have you been in a cave? Harry likes Yu Rang!" said Hermione exasperated.

"What? Ginny's not good enough for you, Harry?"

"Ron!" Hermione yelled appalled. "You are so clueless when it comes to this stuff! There's just no getting through to you!" She grabbed Ron, and despite the fact that he was holding a huge slimy squid, gave him a kiss. Harry felt quite uncomfortable during it. His two best friends kissing, on the lips and everything, yuck! He was greatly relieved when it was over, and pleasantly surprised that Ron was more or less speechless the rest of the night.

As they made their way up to the sixth floor, they passed numerous groups out searching for the Chamber of Cheesecake, too.

When they passed Faco, Shabby, and Foil along with Panties Pimpleton, Faco said with venom in his voice, "Putter!"

Had Faco caught Putter alone, he would have at the very least used his Perfect authority to deduct points from the Nerd house. Since Putter was with Ron and Hermione, they all wordlessly concluded not to bother charging points to each other's group, both casually disregarding the rules.

Harry with equal hate in his voice replied, "Maldoy!"

"What's with Cheesley? He looks like a zombie!"

"He's fine," said Harry derisively.

"Hey Cheesley, is that your girlfriend?

Hermione replied, "Yes."

"Not you, Big Head, I meant the octopus."

They all laughed.

"I'll bet he tried to use that broken wand of his again," added Faco. They all laughed and began walking away.

"Look, I'm Ronald Cheesley, 'ack, ack, ack!'" Faco continued to amuse his goons as he continued down the hall.

When they reached the sixth floor, Shameonus Finnigan and Spleen Davis ran out of a door and slammed it behind them, while yelling in fear. Shameonus's pants were ripped. His leg was bleeding.

"What's wrong?" asked Harry, wand ready.

Spleen said, "There's a vicious dog in there, guarding a trap door. We thought it might lead to the Chamber of Cheesecakes, but we can't get past the beast. We even tried giving it a doggy biscuit, but it was no good."

"Well that's enough for me, I'm going to bed!" said Shameonus, as he limped away.

When they were gone, Harry turned to Hermione and said, "I'll bet the Chamber of Cheesecakes IS past that guard dog. Let's take a peek, shall we?"

"Why not?" replied Hermione. Ron's lips puckered a little.

They cracked open the door, and peered cautiously within. Harry laughed, "It's only a poodle!" The poodle stared at them and growled a bit. Harry relaxed, and opened the door to step in.

"Careful, Harry, poodles can have bad tempers," warned Hermione.

"Hi Girl, don't be afraid," Harry said while slowly entering the room. Hermione held her wand ready, just in case.

"Easy Girl," said Harry, stepping slowly toward the poodle, his empty hand held out for the dog to sniff. It bared its teeth now as it growled loudly, and Hermione was getting nervous.

"Harry, watch out!" she yelled as the poodle launched itself at Harry's throat. "Alpo Purina Iams," but her spell missed the leaping dog.

Harry put up his arm to ward off the vicious poodle. The dog latched painfully onto his wrist, and he dropped his wand.

"Ow, you mangy mutt!"

"Harry get outta there!"

Harry made for the door, dragging the small canine with him. He painfully pulled his arm through the door, as the snarling dog ripped his sleeve from his robe, the seam gave way at the shoulder. Hermione wasn't too happy to see that. It was her spare robe. She had lent it to Harry, since Harry didn't have any of his own things.

"What the...? Did you see that? That thing's from the pits of hell!" yelled Harry.

"Your wand, Harry, you left your wand!"

"She can have it, I'm not going back in there!"

"Don't be an IDIOT! How are you going to defend yourself without your wand? We have to get it back."

She opened the door a crack, the dog growled at her. She readied her wand. Then she flung the door open, and flicked her wand saying, "Fetch!" As the poodle sprinted across the room after her wand, she sprang through the open door, diving for the wand Harry had dropped. She quickly somersaulted to her feet, and ran back to the door. She almost made it through in time, but the angry canine latched onto her pant leg. She balanced on one foot, trying to kick at the dog and pull her leg out the door at the same time. She pulled her leg out of the room with a tearing sound. The poodle thrashed the torn piece of her pant leg. Then she closed the door and leaned back against it sucking wind. "Phwew! I got it, Harry! Now at least you'll have your wand. I'll have to get another as soon as I can."

Harry gave her a look of confusion, "Hermione, have you lost your marbles?"

"What? It was a sacrifice, my wand for yours. You need yours more than I do. At least now you'll be able to defend yourself against all those people who want you dead."

"Let me show you the non-muddle method," said Harry as he shooed her away from the door. He opened it a crack, just like Hermione had done a moment before. The dog was ready, but couldn't reach Harry through the small crack. Harry spoke the summoning charm, "Aamco Premium Gasoline wand!" The wand shot off the floor of the room and landed in Harry's empty hand with a satisfying smack. He closed the door and handed Hermione her wand.

Hermione slapped her forehead, "I'm such an IDIOT!"

Ron stood there holding Nemoy. His lips puckered a little.

When Harry and Ron arrived back in their room, Harry noticed the torn curtain on his four-poster bed. The dummy he had constructed was slashed apart. Someone had tried to kill him.

Chapter 7

Defense against the Fine Arts

The next day, everyone was exhausted. The Great Eatery was almost as quiet as a grave during breakfast. Most had nodded off; some had nodded off in their gruel. The Party Animal House tables were deserted. They had all spent the night at the Electric Underwear. Even when the small National Geographic team arrived, it failed to cause even a stir.

The quiet was interrupted when the goats came bleating in with the morning mail. Hermione received her copy of the Daily Asylum. She put her money in the pouch around the goat's neck. She didn't bother to read it. "No news is good news," she said folding the newspaper over her face to reduce the light. She remained quiet thereafter.

Ron was busy composing a quick note to his mother, "Send more wands! Love Ron." He sealed the envelope then slapped the hindquarters of his miserable old goat, Pigwedgie. It gave him a look of derision, and walked slowly and indignantly away. Then Ron realized he forgot to give it the envelope, and scampered after it.

Harry felt wide-awake as he went over his class schedule. He couldn't sleep a wink last night and he knew he would pay for it later. First was History of Magic with Professor Binge, then

Transmogrification with Minerva McGooglesnot, followed by Defense Against the Fine Arts with Farthard, then lunch. After lunch, it was onward to Astro-Numerology with the centaur Frenzy, Magical Beast Biology with Cubious Hasbeen, How to Saw a Lady in Half and Other Classics with Humphrey the Wise and Mystical, and last, Poisons with his least favorite teacher ever, Carnivorous Ape. Ron and Hermione had similar schedules. They had Conjuring and Illusions, instead of "Sawing".

Without exception, those in attendance, which was noticeably sparse, slept through Harry's first class, History of Magic with Professor Binge. The ghost's droning voice was very conducive to sleep. Afterward, no one could even say what the topic of the lecture had been. Hermione was the only one who felt guilty, and she had the least reason to feel that way, as she already knew the course material in far greater detail than would be studied in class throughout the year.

Everyone was feeling much more awake and refreshed in their second class, Transmogrification with Professor McGooglesnot. She started class off and ended it by repeating her encouragement that the students bring her any cheesecake they came upon.

Because they were all sixth year students, she reminded them that sixth year students always took an overnight class trip to Atlantis in the early spring. She whetted their appetite for the trip, which she ran each year, by talking about the places they would visit. The Neptune Museum, the King's Palace, the Atlantic Aquarium, and the Coliseum were the cultural highlights of the trip. In addition, they would be staying at the famous Parthan Hotel and have dinner at the most exquisite seafood restaurant, The Ambergris Grill. The trip was entirely government-funded. She had already applied for and received approval for this year's grant. The students were very excited.

Then it was down to business. She went over the itinerary. They were expected to be able to transmute lead into gold by the end of the year. She reminded them that the material they learned this year would appear on their Mature Occult Aptitude Tests, or M.O.A.T's, at the end of next year. The students, however, had their own acronym for M.O.A.T's, the Mother Of All Tests. In a sentence, their graduation depended on them learning the material she would be presenting this year.

Then she began reviewing last year's work, endeavoring to shake the rust off that had accrued over the summer months.

As Ron, Harry, and Hermione headed to Defense Against the Fine Arts, they eagerly discussed the trip to Atlantis. Hermione was very excited about the cultural experience. Ron and Harry were hoping to see some mermaids.

That's when they noticed a woman sweeping the hall with a huge dust broom. It was Belch's huge dust broom. The woman was god-awful ugly. In fact, she looked like a man, –an ugly one. The woman stared at them as they went by, in a way that made Harry nervous. Could anyone have a nose like that? She seemed somehow familiar to him. He began wonder if she was the witch Bellatrix Le Deranged, one of the Fungus Eaters.

Gildersneeze Farthard began lisping his lecture, "From what I underthtand, your training over the courthe of the patht five yearth hath been thhamefulwy lacking and woefulwy mithmanaged in regard to Defenthe Againtht the Fine Artth. You have not even had the thame teacher for two yearth in a row. Looking over the lesthonth taught to you, I have found thome very notitheable gapth in your education. I feel it ith my duty to clothe thethe gapth, tho that you are fully prepared to defend yourthelveth thhould the need arithe. Furthermore, I thought it would be really egthiting if we thtarted the year off with a bang, thomething to give you all a good egthample of what you can egthpect this year in MY clath. Tho today'th lesthon will be about the Efreet or evil genie."

It wasn't pretty to watch. Flecks of spittle hit the floorboards as Farthard talked. Harry felt a few droplets, and he was in the third row. He felt sorry for those up front.

Hermione raised her hand, and asked, "Mr. Farthard?"

"Yeth, my dear?"

"Aren't Efreeti rather egthceptional, I mean, exceptional, that is to say rarely to be encountered? Should we be studying something that we are most likely to never encounter in our whole lives, especially considering we haven't even learned to …"

"Dear child," Farthard wiped his lip, "I'm well aware that you have much to learn. Tho, if you pleasthe, I will dethide what gapth need filling and when. Now, ath I wath thaying, Efreet ath you probabwy have heard, can be forthed to therve ath thlaveth for one thouthand dayth by very powerful withardth."

Faco Maldoy whispered to Ron, "That leaveth you out, Cheethley!"

"Go thuck on a lemon, Maldoy!" replied Harry.

Gildersneeze continued, "Like all genieth, Efreeti will generally offer their captor three wistheth in egthchange for their fweedom. However, unlike regular genieth, Efreeti are generalwy vewy nathty and will twy to thwart their captor'th wistheth by adhering to the letter of the wisth inthtead of the thp-p-pirit of the wisth. Tho, one must be vewy careful in the wording of what they wisth for. For egthhample, withhing for gold, the Efreet might bury their captor in gold dutht enough to choke the foolisth withard who wisthed for it to death. Or, thay one wisthhed to be irrethisthtible, imagine all the trouble that poor fool would find himthelf in. The least of hith problemth would be the womcn hc'd have to fight off with a thtick, just imagine when the fisth came fwying out of the lake twying to have a meaningful relationsthhip-p-p with him, and don't think it would thtop there. Boy was I thur…errr, I mean boy, wouldn't he be thurprithed when it turnth out that dragonth would altho be enamored by him, and dragonth are a lot harder to thay no to than fisth! Take it from me, you have to be vewy careful what you wisthh for! Any questionth?"

Half the students raised their hands, Hermione half stood up from her chair to get noticed.

"Well, thince there are no questionth, we can get down to buthinesth. Today, I have an Effreet here for you all to learn about directly. I thhall open itth bottle forthwith," said Farthard as he placed his thumbs on the cork and began pushing it out of the dark bottle.

"Mr. Farthard, isn't that dangerous?" Hermione called out. She knew this was far more dangerous than the mischievous bogglethwarts that Farthard had uncaged the first year he taught them, and that had been a disaster.

"Don't worry, dear, everything ith under control."

"But, shouldn't we inscribe pentagrams on the floor for protection first?" suggested Hermione as she wiped her eye.

"Really not nethesthary," scoffed Gildersneeze, "a powerful withard thuch as mythelf ith no match for an Efreet. How do you think it got in thith bottle in the firtht plathe?" Gildersneeze turned the bottle and tried pushing the cork from the other side.

"Didn't it come that way?" asked Hermione.

"What, do you think, it was born in a bottle?" jeered Farthard.

The students laughed, and Faco whispered, "Thtop being thuch a baby, Thtranger."

"Grow up," she retorted. She knew Farthard was a bumbling idiot. He had most likely gotten the Efreet from a mail order catalog. He was most likely in way over his head. She seemed to be the only one who had a clue just how much danger they all were in.

"Now, if you were doing thith alone, I would recommend that you firtht of all not do it alone, and thecondly…mmmmfph," he gritted his teeth as he pulled at the cork, "thinthe you aren't a powerful withard, you would definitely want the protection of a pentagram," he finished as he finally popped the cork out. There was a loud bang and billowing black smoke rocketed out of the bottle. The recoil knocked Farthard on his rear end.

The smoke cleared a bit, revealing a genie. His muscular torso looked perfectly formed, as though sculpted. He floated on a jet of black smoke where one might expect his waist and legs to be. The Efreet had dark red skin and flaming hair. He stretched and yawned showing a full array of sharp black teeth.

"Ah, children. Delicious!" he said. His deep, booming voice alone was enough to scare the bejeezus out of the students. They sat frozen in horror. Then he turned to size up the puny human holding his bottle, and getting up off the floor. The thread of spittle sliding down the human weakling's chin made it look imbecilic.

"You must be a powerful wizard indeed to teach such tender morsels about the Efreeti." The thread of drool sliding down the evil genie's chin made it look hungry. His spittle singed the floorboards.

Gildersneeze bowed at the compliment.

"Therefore, in return for my freedom, I will grant you three wishes! But you must make them quickly, I haven't got all day," effected the Efreet slyly.

The students were fooled, and some quickly forgot their fear at the offer of three wishes. A lot of them cheered, and a few began shouting out wishes to Farthard.

"Wish for a mansion!"

"No, a trip to Wizard World!"

"How bout a Ferrari!"

"Ten billion chocolate slugs!"

With momentary horror Harry thought, what if Farthard wished for his memory back? Harry would be so up the creek.

Gildersneeze started to think it over carefully. One had to be very careful when wording a wish. He was totally unprepared when the jolt of electricity suddenly arced from the Efreet's spread fingers to himself, running over his body and through it, then disbursing through the air to all the students, making them shudder.

As suddenly as it came, the electricity went. The students sat totally silent with their hair standing on end, the only noise that could be heard was Perverti Pickel's gum as it fell out of her mouth onto her desk.

The silence was interrupted when Ron said, "Ow, my fillings are hot!" Then others began to cry and whimper, but most were too shocked to move. The Efreet started shooting blinding fireworks forth from his hands; the bright flashes preventing anyone from seeing what was happening. When the fireworks finally stopped, and after blinking several times, the students' vision finally began to clear. They saw the Efreet now larger than a mountain troll and standing on legs now, with one crushing foot on Farthard's chest, pinning the fool painfully to the floor.

"What should we do?" asked Hermione.

"It's a longsthhot, but pray to whatever god you worsthhip to thave uth!" coughed Gildersneeze. Many of the students began praying. Hermione, Ron, and Harry were not among them.

Harry stepped forward, wand ready, with Ron and Hermione there to support him. "Not so fast, Efreet! You may have defeated our stupid teacher, but you haven't beaten the students yet!" yelled Harry. The Efreet laughed until tears started rolling down his hot cheeks and instantly evaporating.

"Give it your best shot, tender mortal!" growled the evil genie waiting.

Harry summoning all of his power, flicked his wand while saying, "Raid kills bugs dead!"

There was a fizzling pop at the tip of Harry's wand, and for a moment nothing happened. Then slowly the Efreet started to turn to smoke as a gust of wind began whirling around the classroom. Glowing sparks began to appear within the smoke, and the wind became stronger, whipping the students' hair and robes. The Efreet was evaporating into whirling smoke, gradually disappearing. The sparks began to circle in the wind. Loose papers started blowing and circling the room, too.

Hermione yelled to Harry, "Wow, what spell is this?"

The wind grew stronger, students began to cling to their desks or swirl around the room too. "I'll tell you later, if we live!" yelled Harry. He was swept from his feet and began whirling around the room as a tornado formed at its center. The Efreet was gone now, and soon everything in the room, children, desks, and chairs were whirling around and around, higher and higher. Then everything was sucked into the Efreet's bottle as it spun on the floor. The last item, the cork lodged itself tightly in the neck of the dark bottle with a whump. The bottle came to a rest standing up.

They were inside the bottle, and everything was still. Everyone was so small that the bottle seemed incredibly large and more like a well-furnished studio apartment, except for the huge messy pile of children, desks, chairs, and other odds and ends in the center of the spacious room. Harry noticed Ron's wand was further broken. Ron seemed unaware.

"Seems your teacher neglected to tell you that Efreeti are immune to magic spells," laughed the Efreet. "Now you will be MY slaves for a thousand days!"

He began commanding them to their duties. He started by assigning several of the students to toss the mess of desks, chairs, and garbage in the fireplace and burn it. Hermione was lucky she was told to begin fanning the Efreet with a giant palm frond. Harry and Ron weren't so lucky, they were told to start washing and waxing a huge fleet of cars in the garage. However, that wasn't nearly as bad as the job given to Shabby and Foil, Faco Maldoy's two muscular friends. They were told to start marinating themselves in the kitchen.

Once everyone was busy at work, the Efreet settled down on a beautiful divan, propped his feet up on a pillow and started to snooze. A little while later he started to snore. Hermione continued to fan him, keeping a close eye on the genie until she felt sure he wasn't faking. Then she loudly whispered, "Good work, Farthard! That was really impressive!"

"Not to worry, I'm thinking of a plan to get uth out of here," replied the teacher.

"It looks like you're scrubbing the floor," replied Foil sitting in a huge roasting pan next to Shabby and using a baster to shower himself with marinade.

"I've got it!" said Farthard. "I'll thhrink the cork in the bottle, then we can get out while the Efreet thleepth. Go get everyone back in here."

When everyone had gathered back in the main studio, Farthard took out his wand, waved it at the cork high above, and said, "Onomatopoeia!" The cork shrunk until it was too small to stopper the bottle. Unfortunately, the cork was still enormous to them in their shrunken size. It fell heavily on the sleeping Efreet, instantly waking the evil genie.

Before the genie realized what was going on, the kids were throwing themselves upon him like a pack of snarling mad wolverines, biting, pinching, scratching, and kicking. The Efreet was clearly more than a match for any individual, but was unable to do anything about the children. For each one he tossed or kicked off of him, two more jumped back on and he suffered the continuous rage of their combined attack. His only escape was to change back to a puff of smoke. The smoke swirled and sparkled again, and soon everyone was rocketing out of the bottle. They were restored to their former size and were back in the now barren classroom. All were grateful that the Efreet was alone in his bottle, none more so than the evil genie himself.

"WHOO HOO! That was the best class ever!" shouted Faco Maldoy. Most everyone excitedly agreed. Harry, Ron, and Hermione of course couldn't agree with anything Maldoy said, though Harry and Ron each thought it really had been cool. Only Hermione felt that the lesson had been entirely too dangerous, and that they were all lucky to be alive.

"Egthellent clasth, egthellent! I can thee you learned a lot today!" replied Farthard.

"I'm starving," said Ron, "let's go see if we can find something to eat."

"Yeah, " replied Hermione, "we're late for lunch."

Chapter 8

The Err of Slipperin

They arrived in the Great Eatery as lunch was finishing up. That's when they found out the big news. Ape was telling all his classes about Sloberic Slipperin and the Chamber of Cheesecakes. Preschool Nerd Rusty Pipes and Ginny confirmed it. They had little time to talk to Harry, Ron, and Hermione before their next classes began, but they had enough time to let them know the most important facts. The Chamber of Cheesecakes was indeed the work of Sloberic Slipperin, and no, Ginny Cheesley wasn't possessed by an evil cheesecake recipe book.

Ron asked, "If she was possessed by an evil cheesecake recipe book, isn't that just what she would say?"

No one bothered to answer him.

"I heard that you won the Fry-Wizard Tournament, Harry. Is it true?" asked Rusty.

"Well, yeah," replied Harry. He didn't like to talk about it. It brought up painful memories.

"Wow! And you had to answer the Riddle of the Sphinx?"

"Yeah," sighed Harry.

"Wow! Can I have your autograph?" Rusty held out his notebook.

"Sure."

Harry signed Rusty's notebook. As he did, Rusty said, "You'll have to tell me all about it later sometime, I got to get to class."

Harry handed Rusty back his notebook.

"Wow, thanks!" Rusty skipped off to class.

Meanwhile, Ginny handed Ron a package. "It's from Mom," she explained. "Pigwedgie was wandering around earlier, so I took the package for you."

Ron opened the package. Inside there were a few wands and a note. "Thank God," he said out loud.

He opened the note. It read:

> *Do you think these grow on trees?*
> *Love,*
> *Mom*

Meanwhile, Harry was relieved that there was a long row of tables between Ginny and himself. There was no sense in upsetting Ron, especially since he wasn't interested in his sister. When Ginny left, she merely blew him a kiss. Fortunately, Ron was busy and didn't notice.

They quickly ate something that felt like, tasted like, and they strongly suspected were cardboard triangles smothered in cheese sauce. Then, they crossed a rickety rope bridge over a pit of acid to get to their next class, Astro-Numberology.

Frenzy's classroom had an elaborate illusion that made it appear as though you were in the Forbidden Forest of Sure Death, the centaur's home. The primal noises of the forest created a disturbingly chilling atmosphere to learn in.

Frenzy had begun teaching last year, and relished the opportunity to teach human children of the failures of their race. He had a certain knack for making it seem as though they were responsible for all the generations of humans that had preceded them.

In his first lesson, he pointed out that five in numerology was the number that corresponded to woe and misery. Humans having five toes on each foot, stood upon the earth forming a basis for calamity. They were remiss in having bothered to stand up in the first place. Everything that followed in his lecture was even more depressing.

Magical Beast Biology was their next class, taught by Cubious Hasbeen, the Keeper of the Schools Magical Petting Zoo. They headed out the back door of the school, and walked past Lake Iwannabealifeguard, down the path to the log cabin, next to the Magical Creature Petting Zoo, and on the edge of the Forbidden Forest of Sure Death. Vultures circled overhead ominously. The weather was warm and the lake looked beautiful. Harry wished he could cut class and relax in one of the chaise lounges out by the diving board. Maybe there would be time to relax after classes were done for the day.

Harry greeted his good friend Hasbeen warmly.

"'ello 'arry," replied the massive man. Hasbeen always reminded Harry of a large grizzly bear that had escaped the circus wearing a small circus tent. It was probably because Hasbeen got his clothing from Omar the Tent Man's Big and Tall Fashions, that, and all the hair. Completing the image, when he patted Harry on the back, it was like being swatted by a massive paw, knocking Harry to the ground. Hasbeen, like a grizzly bear, didn't know his own strength.

He wasted no time getting the students to work. This year, they would be getting much deeper into magical creatures, spleen deep. Their first project was dissecting a pixie.

"Blech!" Hermione whispered, "Why do they always schedule this class so soon after lunch?"

Harry whispered back, "Would you prefer to do this before lunch?"

Harry found himself anxious in "Sawing" class. Humphrey the Wise and Mystical was demonstrating slight of hand tricks, pulling cards out of thin air. For once in his life, Harry wanted to be in Poisons class, and it seemed like it would never come.

When the gong rang, he dashed from "Sawing" class, running through the hallways, and sliding down the east corridor firepole. Enchilada Johnson called out to him, but he didn't bother to stop. Enchilada Johnson was the Nerd Quibbage Team captain. Most likely she wanted to tell Harry when their first practice would be. He'd find out later. He wanted to get to Poisons class before Ape started talking about the Chamber of Cheesecakes. Harry had a lot of questions, and any clue Professor Ape could give them about the chamber might help solve the mystery. Perhaps Ape even knew how to get past the poodle and might accidentally let the information slip.

He stopped to catch his breath outside the dungeon laboratory where Carnivorous Ape taught Poisons. He was not the first anxious student to arrive. He was however, the least prepared student to arrive.

When he entered, Ape sneered, "Putter, where is your cauldron?" No "hello," no "welcome back," no warm or welcoming smile.

"Hello Professor, it's good to see you again, did you have a pleasant holiday?"

"Never mind that, Putter, your cauldron?"

"Errr, I don't have one. I don't have any of my equipment, 'cept for my wand."

"Putter, you are sorely wrong if you think I want to hear any of your sob stories."

Hermione and Ron dashed in, out of breath. It was obvious they had been running in the halls.

Ape turned on them. "Running in the halls, are we, Mr. Perfect, and Ms. Perfect? A fine example you set for the rest of the students. That's minus five points for each of you, for running, and minus five more for setting a poor example."

Faco and his groupies walked in just in time to hear Ape subtract points from the Nerds House. Ron and Hermione had run past them in the hall. He smiled pleasantly, and greeted the professor. Then he coolly announced, "Not only were they running in the halls, but they knocked down one of the preschoolers. I had to help the little girl up, and send her to the hospital wing. Hopefully her cut won't need stitches."

"What?" Hermione raised her voice indignantly.

"Liar!" accused Ron.

"That's enough!" commanded the professor. "That's minus five more points for each of you! Now take your seats!"

"Oh, and Putter, minus five points for you, too, for not being prepared. Have your equipment ready, or I'll subtract ten next time."

Harry opened his mouth to explain that he didn't have any of his equipment, that it was all back home at Privy Drive. Ape cut him off, pointing and saying, "Shut it."

The professor began class by asking review questions from last year's studies. "Who can tell me what poisonous substance can be used to cure lycanthropy?"

Hermione was the only one to raise her hand high. Ape called on Harry.

Harry swallowed. "Garlic?"

Ape growled, "Putter, I do believe that another series of Remedial Potions work is in order, you will stay after class."

When Ape mentioned Remedial Potions work after class, Harry knew right away that Ape really meant something else entirely. "Remedial Potions" was the code phrase Harry and he had worked out last year for their secret after class activity. In accordance with Grumblesnore's request, Harry began studying with Professor Ape after school last year. Grumblesnore thought Harry would benefit greatly from yoga. He was concerned about Harry's ability to channel Lord Moldyfart. It usually happened at night, and at first Harry thought he was dreaming. Later it became clear at moments Harry was able to see what Lord Moldyfart could see, hear what Lord Moldyfart could hear, and feel what the Fart Lord felt. Grumblesnore was concerned this ability would eventually become known to the Fart Lord, and when it did, Lord Moldyfart was sure to try to use it to his advantage. Grumblesnore decided that yoga was just the thing. Yoga would have a calming influence on Harry, and help the high-strung boy keep his mind clear, at peace, and inside its own thick skull. Harry naturally disliked yoga, it represented everything the hyperboy drama queen was not. However, it was obvious from Ape's comment that Grumblesnore wanted Harry to continue practicing yoga this year with Ape after school. Harry wished Ape would call it "Honors Potion" work instead of "Remedial Potion" work. However, Ape's code phrase was a lot more realistic and attracted no suspicion whatsoever.

Harry turned red.

"Anyone else?" He deliberately ignored Hermione's waving arm.

"Faco?"

"Belladonna."

"Correct, also known as nightshade."

After a series of similar review questions, Ape waved his wand and a complex series of instructions appeared on the chalkboard. They were instructions for brewing a concoction that was poisonous to humans, but was excellent fertilizer for growing lotus blossoms, a very useful ingredient in many other deadly poisons and antidotes.

Harry was balking inside. Why was Ape teaching class? Why wasn't Ape telling them about the Chamber of Cheesecakes? He had told all of his other classes the whole story, why wasn't he telling them? His questions were clogging his brain, preventing him from concentrating. They were on the tip of his tongue, but he couldn't ask. He didn't want to give Ape the satisfaction.

Fortunately, someone else came to his rescue. Perverti Pickle raised her hand, and when the professor acknowledged her, she asked, "But, aren't you going to tell us about the Chamber of Cheesecakes?"

"You are all sixth year students. You were here when the Chamber of Frozen Dairy Desserts was opened. Or have you forgotten already?"

Pickle blushed. "No, of course not, but …"

"Well, then what do you wish to know? I'm sure you have already heard that Sloberic Slipperin is the wizard responsible for both of these dessert chambers?"

"But, …"

Ape sighed. "All right, for those of you who may have been brainfreezed last time, I'll review the events that took place during your second year."

"It was on the first day of school that Belch's cat, Chuck Norris, was found incapacitated. It had licked a bowl of ice cream. Ice cream that had come from the Chamber of Frozen Dairy Desserts. The cat was instantly brainfreezed. Above it there was a message. It was just like the one you saw yesterday above Belch, only, it was about ice cream and ice cream sandwiches and such, not cheesecakes.

Now, if you recall, I explained to you back then about Sloberic Slipperin. He was one of the founders of this school, and the creator of the Chamber of Frozen Dairy Desserts. No one knows why exactly, the guy was just insane about dessert for some reason. He loved his desserts. And I suppose he got sick and tired of little children with no respect for rules raiding the school's freezers and taking his desserts without permission. It's just one more example of how much happier we would all be if everyone obeyed the rules. Anyway, he's the one who set up the Chamber of Frozen Dairy Desserts, to protect his ice cream and ice cream novelties. He set up the chamber both to protect his desserts and to keep them magically fresh forever. And he created a key to open the chamber, so that his heir, the Heir of Slipperin, would be able to enjoy his legacy."

He paused to spell "Heir" on the chalkboard.

"If you'll recall, the Heir of Slipperin arrived that day, four years ago. Someone brought a cookbook for Frozen Dairy Desserts in to school. The cookbook was the key that opened up the hidden chamber, and started the whole fiasco with cats and students getting brainfreezed and all.

"Finally, one of the students destroyed the cookbook, resealing the Chamber of Frozen Dairy Desserts. Those who were brainfreezed were eventually defrosted and have since, fully recovered.

Quite obviously Sloberic's insanity didn't end there. He apparently has set up other hidden dessert chambers within the school, well, at least one other chamber. This latest one seems to put out some pretty awesome cheesecake. However, it looks like the result is virtually the same, once you eat it, you're finished, that is, stuck in the hospital wing for a good long time."

"So what does it all mean?" asked Faco.

"It means, that the key to the Chamber of Cheesecakes has arrived, someone probably has brought a cookbook in, one with cheesecake recipes. It means that the Err of Slipperin has arrived." He paused to write down "Err" on the chalkboard.

"Or to be more exact, The Heir of the Err of Slipperin has arrived. It is well documented that Sloberic Slipperin's first child, Salvador Slipperin was brilliant like his father. However, against his better judgment, he and his wife decided to have a second child, who turned out to be, quite stupid. In fact, Sloberic was greatly embarrassed by his second son, whose real name ironically was Solomon. He used to refer to Solomon as Simpleton instead. While Salvador was his heir, Simpleton was his err." He pointed to the two words on the chalkboard as he spoke.

"Any questions?"

"I don't get it," said Lavatory Brown. "What's, like, the big deal? Like, so what if a room full of cheesecake suddenly, like, pops open? I mean, like, wouldn't that be a good thing? Like, especially if you, like, like cheesecake?"

"Ms. Brown, what it means is that we are all once again in great danger. The Chamber of Frozen Dairy Desserts was guarded by a hideous and quite deadly monster. I'm sure that we can expect no less, this time."

Ape slapped the desk in front of him to get their attention.

"Let me make myself clear. Under no circumstances, should any of you attempt to find this Chamber of Cheesecakes! It is far too dangerous. And that goes double for you, Putter!"

Elvis Grumblesnore walked into Poisons class a moment before the gong rang signaling that class was over. He looked at Harry and said, "I'd like to have a word with you, Harry, if I may?"

"Sure," said Harry, happy for any excuse that would get him out of doing yoga with Ape. Grumblesnore led Harry to his office and held back the bead curtain for Harry to enter.

Inside Grumblesnore's office, Harry's eyes raced from one interesting artifact to the next. The walls were covered with gold records. There was a glamorous black leather outfit including sunglasses in a glass class on the wall behind Grumblesnore's desk. There was a white outfit with sequins and a cape on an Elvis mannequin. It had plastic lei garlands around the neck. There was an acoustic guitar on a stand in the corner, next to ancient-looking microphone on a stand.

On the desk, there was a metal colander, a half-eaten peanut butter and banana sandwich, and Elvis's pet rock, Raukes. Elvis was fond of saying "Raukes Rocks!"

An elf was hard at work washing the windows. It turned to look at Harry for a second, but didn't greet him. It was Bobby. Bobby was pretending not to know Harry in front of Grumblesnore. Harry wondered about this. Why would Bobby hide his pretense of friendship with Harry from Grumblesnore? Bobby was afraid of something, but what? Was he afraid Grumblesnore would find out about Bobby's hatred for Harry?

Grumblesnore asked Harry to sit, then walked behind his desk and sat down in his own seat. He picked up the colander from the desk, and placed it inverted on his own head. Harry was already familiar with Grumblesnore's magical colander. It had a triple purpose; it improved Grumblesnore's memory, it kept extra-terrestrials from reading his mind, and of course, it could be used in the traditional way, to strain pasta.

"Well, Harry, welcome back," began Elvis. "I hope you had a nice summer. Feeling any better about your deceased uncle?"

Harry felt a sudden pang and stuttered, "I-I-I think about him all the time. Everything reminds me of him."

"That's quite normal. It takes time to get over these things. Time will heal your wounds Harry. The key is to stay busy. Busy doing good things, like studying, playing quibbage, and practicing your yoga."

Harry eyed the unfinished sandwich on the desk. He sighed, "Must I continue with yoga? It isn't working, I'm no good at it."

"He who masters yoga, masters himself. If it were only possible, I would have you practicing yoga twelve hours each day. However, since it isn't, I want you to continue to train everyday with Professor

Ape after class, and I want you to practice what he teaches each night before you go to bed. Or, if you prefer, we could try Ritalin?"

Harry slumped in his chair. "No, thanks."

He continued to eye the half sandwich on Grumblesnore's desk. Harry had the feeling it knew something important. What did it know?

"I heard what Professor Ape said to you. 'Under no circumstances should you search for the Chamber of Cheesecakes.' I have to agree with him, Harry. You really must learn to keep your nose out of situations that are not your concern. You've got enough on your plate already being the enemy of the Fart Lord. You should leave the Chamber of Cheesecakes to me."

Enough on his plate, enough on his plate. Harry had been staring at the half sandwich on the plate. He looked up and said, "Huh?"

"I mean it Harry. It's for your own good. You've walked a very fine line in the past, and I'm sorry, but if you cross it this time, I'm afraid I'm going to have to expel you."

"Expel me!"

"Yes, Harry, expel. It's time for you to grow up. The rules apply to even you. If you are caught outside your quarters after curfew, regretfully, that will be the end of your stay here."

"What if there is an attempt on my life? May I leave my quarters if someone is trying to kill me?" His knee began to bounce up and down. Harry just needed a distraction, any distraction, so that he could have a minute alone with that sandwich.

"Harry, calm down. The Fart Lord cannot enter the school. His fungus eaters are all on the run. No one here is trying to kill you. You are safe, safer than you would be at home."

"But just in case, someone is trying to talk to me, I mean, kill me..." Harry couldn't take his eyes off the sandwich. Beads of perspiration broke out on his brow. He was losing control.

"Please stop looking for loopholes. Is there someone else trying to kill you?"

It was Harry's big chance. Whenever an opportunity to ask for help came, Harry never took it. The most recent was last spring, if he had asked Ape for help, perhaps his uncle, Serious Smack the Clown, would still be alive. Perhaps all the Fungus Eaters would have been arrested instead of escaping. Now was his big chance, he could tell Grumblesnore about the conspiracy to kill him, he could prove it, all he had to do was show Grumblesnore the official Hogwashes notice that school had been canceled.

Harry replied, "No." He barely knew what he was saying, all he could think about was the sandwich and what important information it knew.

"Well then, isn't that question rather moot?"

Harry couldn't stop himself, he began talking to the sandwich in morsel-tongue. "Hey, sandwich wake up! Tell me what you know!"

Grumblesnore's eyes widened. He couldn't understand what Harry was saying, but he knew what was happening. He grabbed the remaining half of his peanut butter and banana sandwich and without a word, crammed the entire thing in his mouth.

Chapter 9

Searching for the Err

Over the next month, everyone was trying to find out who the Heir of the Err of Slipperin was. Everyone was on the lookout for the cookbook containing cheesecake recipes, but none was found.

Harry was convinced that it had to be Faco Maldoy. It all made sense. Faco was stupid, just like Simpleton Slipperin; therefore, he had to be the Heir of the Err. It had long been a principle of Harry, Ron, and Hermione's to pin any wrongdoing or bad situation on their enemy, Maldoy, whether guilty or not, especially if there was even the remotest chance of getting Faco in trouble. It would be especially satisfying if Faco turned out to be a direct descendent of the Err of Slipperin, however, completely unnecessary to their way of thinking.

Yet, even Maldoy wasn't stupid enough to openly admit that he was the direct descendent of a moron. Harry, Ron, and Hermione needed a way to find out. However, a way to find out eluded them.

Quite similarly, many of his fellow students suspected Harry was the Heir to the Err. This Harry fervently denied, though inwardly, he wondered if it could be himself. Tom Riddly was the Heir of Slipperin after all. If his enemy was the Heir of Slipperin, wouldn't it make sense if he were the Heir of the Err? He hoped not. If they ever held a family reunion, it sure would be awkward.

During this time, there had been four cheesecake incidents. All involved a student randomly coming across a cheesecake buying opportunity. A cheesecake vending machine would appear in some lonely corridor. The student would insert their twelve galleys to make their purchase. (Every student and teacher carried at least twelve galleys in case they were blessed with such an opportunity. Some carried as much as 144 galleys around with them, ready to buy a dozen such cheesecakes.) Each student then selected his or her favorite cheesecake. Students licked their lips as the variety was described to them. There was the classic plain cheesecake. It was by itself truly scrumptious without adding other flavors to the experience. There was strawberry cheesecake, topped with real fresh strawberries in a strawberry glaze. There was sinful Belgian chocolate. There was luscious caramel, gooey and sweet. Finally, there was succulent raspberry truffle. Five magnificent kinds in all.

Each victim, as though in a daze, took the box from the vending machine and carefully opened it, just to see what it looked like, mind you. They had every intention of buying several more, sharing them with others, selling slices at a huge profit, using a fork and plate, and turning a piece in to Professor McGooglesnot for all those House Cup points. (She had raised her offer to two thousand points.) All their plans were dashed when each, carefully took a pinch, just to try it, mind you. However, no one could recall exactly what came over them or what happened next, though it was obvious to all. They simple went out of their minds, scooping up handfuls of the cheesecake, or plowing their faces directly into their purchase until only crumbs remained, if that.

Each victim was found later by some passerby. The vending machine would be long gone. All that would remain would be the prostrate victim lying next to a box holding an empty pie tin. The passerby invariably snarfed up any loose crumbs, then called for help. Such good Samaritans that were unlucky enough to find a crumb, suffered doubly. For only they truly knew, exactly what they were missing. They became the most obsessed about finding cheesecake.

Like Belch, all four victims were still in the hospital ward. At first, they were incapacitated with fullness of stomach. A day later, they were unable to eat anything that wasn't cheesecake. They were driven to tears at the thought of eating anything else ever again, especially anything prepared by Henry, the head Kitchen-Elf. They would have wasted away, if not fed intravenously.

Ever since the first attempt on his life, Harry had continued to make a dummy in his bed at night. However, his pillow had been shredded, as well as an assortment of Ron's clothes. He needed something else to make a dummy out of. That's when Harry decided that he would use Grumblesnore's Elvis mannequin. He "borrowed" it when Grumblesnore wasn't around. He kept it under his bed during the day, and at night, he would place it in the bed, and sleep under Ron's bed. When he woke up the next morning, invariably he would find the dummy in worse shape than he left it the night before. Sometimes the unknown assailant would leave their weapon behind. In fact, Harry was accumulating quite a collection. He found guns, knives, swords, fire pokers, a cricket bat, a golf club, and a war axe. When he went down to breakfast, he was usually greeted by stares of disbelief. For by then, usually a rumor had spread that he was dead.

Grumblesnore was quite angry that someone had removed his Elvis mannequin from his office. "Is nothing sacred?" he asked. Harry thought Grumblesnore would be very happy to know that it was being used to save his life nightly. However, he wasn't about to admit his responsibility for the abduction.

As long as the weather was good, Harry and Ron practiced with the rest of their quibbage team daily after classes and after Harry was done with 'Remedial Poisons.' Sometimes practice went on after dark. While they practiced, Hermione usually expounded on the virtues of being elf-less to anyone who would listen to her. Anyone foolish enough to do so, never did twice. If it weren't for the fact that Ron was busy with quibbage practice, he may have been forced to join the OSPREE Club, as it was, Hermione was still the only member. It was clear that Hermione directed their relationship, though Ron for some reason refused to admit that they were even going out, citing the fact that he had never asked Hermione to go anywhere with him. He insisted they were not dating. They were obviously a couple to everyone except Ron.

Harry felt awkward and uncomfortable many times around them. There were times when he felt like he was intruding on a private moment. Their snuggling started to repulse him. Cripes, couldn't they save it for when he wasn't around?

To make matters worse, Harry noticed that Yu Rang and Michael Coronary had become a couple. They were always holding hands in the halls. How could she want him for a boyfriend? Blech.

Meanwhile, Harry sent a letter to the Dirtleys asking them to send his trunk of clothing and other possessions. A week later, Harry sent a letter begging them to send his things. A week later, Harry told Hasbeen about his problem. The next day, Hasbeen delivered Harry's trunk, and his pet goat, Headbutt. Harry was elated.

"I hope you gave them all a serious thrashing," Harry said scornfully.

"Don't worry 'bout that. I'm sure if you send 'em any more letters, next time, tha'll answer right quick," the big man replied.

Harry had his trunk and most of his possessions. He had his dungbombs, silly string, farting underpants, ultra-burp soda, butt-enlarging crackers, fake wands, a dribble goblet of fire, ventrilo-whoopy cushions, glue-gum, and mace-squirting flowers. The only important item missing was his cauldron. Hasbeen must have missed it. Harry cursed his luck. However, at least he finally had some clothes to change into, and most importantly, he had his special cloak and map. He immediately went on a spree of mischief, planting his ventrilo-whoopy cushions in the Nerd House Common Room, substituting fake wands for real ones, and offering gum, soda, and crackers to all his Nerd friends.

When the weekend trip to Hogsbreath came around, he restocked his favorite prank items at Fred and George's joke shop. He bought some of the anti-matter toothpaste, they had invented, too. It was a hoot.

He also bought a cell phone at the new Cingular shop in Hogsbreath.

"What do you need a cell phone for?" asked Hermione.

"I don't know, I just couldn't resist. Maybe I'll call Uncle Vermin, and ask him if his refrigerator is running," Harry laughed.

Hermione rolled her eyes. Hopefully, Harry would get over this incredibly stupid phase soon.

Once Harry had his cloak and map, Ron, Hermione, and he made several attempts to get past the poodle. Harry risked being expelled. However, with his cloak and map, there was little chance of being caught. Several times they had passed Gretchen Shoemacker, the new school custodian, Belch's ugly replacement, in the halls. She seemed just as eager as Belch to catch students up after curfew. However, she was no smarter than Belch, and easily fooled.

During one attempt, Ron brought Nemoy along. The dog was indifferent to the squid, but was clearly vicious to humans.

Each attempt to get past the poodle only made them more afraid of it. They concluded that it was futile. Their only hope was to find out who the Heir to the Err was, and find out how to get past the dog from them. Unfortunately, Ginny showed no signs of being possessed by an evil cheesecake recipe book. She was one of the few that they could scratch off their list of potential suspects.

Maldoy was at the top of the list, and it was quickly becoming important to Harry that they make some progress. Harry wanted proof one way or another. Either Maldoy was the Heir of the Err or he wasn't. He decided to interview the remains of Faco's meals. He soon discovered that Shabby and Foil usually ate anything Faco left behind. Harry planted bowls of oatmeal around Faco's favorite table in the Great Eatery, Shabby and Foil ate these too. Finally, one day, he recovered a bowl half-filled with oatmeal. Unfortunately, it knew nothing. Harry decided it was time for more drastic measures.

So late one early October evening, Harry, Ron, and Hermione decided to use Harry's special cloak to do a little snooping around. Ron had to be told to put his squid, Nemoy, back in its tank. Neither Harry nor Hermione wanted to be under the cloak with a slimy cephalopod mollusk. It was bad enough being under the cloak with Ron.

The cloak was special not just because it had been his late father's cloak, but also because of its more significant properties. The cloak was actually a large sheet with two eyeholes cut out. Anyone using the cloak looked like a ghost. Using the cloak they were able to travel the haunted and hallowed halls of Hogwashes, indistinguishable from the other specters that roamed freely about, such as Nearly Earless Nick, Peeved the Poltergeist, or the Muddy Cruddy Baron. The only difference was the three sets of sneakers squeaking down the halls underneath. The cloak was better than being invisible. People might have accidentally bump into them if they were invisible. Wearing the sheet, everyone got out of their way, most with a bewildered expression.

They worked their way down to the dungeon and eventually stood outside the entrance to the Popular Rich Kids House. Harry checked to make sure the coast was clear, and then removed the sheet. The entrance was guarded by a portrait of a silly-looking man with bloodshot-eyes. The portrait asked, "Password?"

To this Harry raised his index and middle fingers in a <u>V</u> and quickly jabbed at the man's bloodshot eyes.

However, the man in the portrait was quicker, and blocked Harry with one hand, while saying in a squeaky voice, "Oh, a wise guy!" Then he slapped all three of them across their faces with one sweep of his hand.

Harry started to panic, what was the next step? Was he supposed to give the man a nuggie or box his ear? He felt like such a stooge. Hermione reached into the portrait and grabbed hold of the man's ear twisting it.

"Thanks," whispered Harry, remembering the sequence now.

"OH, HOO, HOO!" cried the man in the portrait.

"Say Uncle!" said Hermione with a note of victory in her voice.

"Uncle!" squeaked the high-pitched voice of the silly-looking man. The portrait swung open, and Hermione let go of the man's ear.

They were in, and were secretly all very pleased to have gotten into the Popular Rich Kid House so easily. Little did they realize that just beyond the portrait was an entrance foyer with a state-of-the-art security system. Its synthetic female voice pleasantly requested, "Please position your chin on the bar for Retina Scan Comparison."

Harry looked at Ron who shrugged. Harry exploded, "Oh, great! I thought you said you knew how to get in! Cheesley you are such a moron!"

"Me? If it weren't for me, you wouldn't have made it this far! You should be thanking me, Putter, you idiot!" shouted Ron.

"What good is getting this far, we can't get by this! And as far as idiots go, your village called and said their idiot is missing!"

"Well, you're so stupid you get scammed all the time by the village idiot!" retorted Ron.

Hermione interjected, "All right! That's enough!" She grabbed their ears and twisted.

Ron and Harry immediately doubled over in pain. They stopped shouting at each other, shouting, "OOH, HOO, HOO!" instead.

"I surprised at the both of you! Do you know how childish you sound with all that name-calling? You guys know we're on the same team, and all this bickering isn't going to help us get by this retina scanner! Now shake hands and apologize!"

She let go of their ears.

With bashful reluctance, Harry said, "Sorry Ron, you did great getting us in this far." He held out his hand to Ron.

Ron shook it saying, "No problem, pal, I'm sorry too, I didn't hear anything about this thing. I guess I should have tried to find out more."

Hermione seemed satisfied and said, "Now if you two sloth-brained Neanderthals are finished, can we try to figure out a way to get in there?"

Just then the muffled request of, "Password?" could be heard from the portrait immediately outside. Ron, Harry, and Hermione scrambled to get under the sheet before whoever was outside found them in a very compromising spot. "Oh, man! If that's Professor Ape, we are so busted!" whispered Hermione.

"Oh crap, Hermione, why did you have to say that? I think I just messed my pants," said Ron quietly.

The portrait swung open to the cursing of the guy in the portrait, and Faco Maldoy stepped inside. The synthetic female voice pleasantly requested, "Please position your chin on the bar for Retina Scan Comparison."

"Holy Crap! A Ghost!" cried Maldoy. "And one without designer sheets. You must be in the wrong house," he concluded.

"Cough, errr, I'm the ghost of Shabby. This is where I belong," said Harry affecting a deep and spooky-sounding voice.

Shabby stepped into the foyer behind Faco. The synthetic female voice pleasantly repeated its request.

"I mean, Foil."

"Foil! Oh no! I didn't even know you were sick!" cried Faco.

"Uh, I drank poison in Poisons class by mistake. I thought it was grape juice," Harry explained.

"Oh man! What a bummer. Can I have your hoverboard?" asked Shabby.

"Yeah, I guess. By the way, are either of you the Err of Slipperin?" asked Harry.

"Me? Nah, if I was the Err of Slipperin, I'd sell the recipe book to a big cheesecake company for a million dollars!" said Maldoy. Shabby laughed as he headed over to the Retina Scan bar.

"Okay, then, see you, I just remembered, I forgot to do something," said Harry. The three pair of sneakers started to hightail it out of there.

"When's the funeral?" asked Faco, calling out after them.

"Wednesday."

Chapter 10

The Quibbage Match

It is said that inspiration struck Elvis Grumblesnore when he accidentally stepped in a pile left by one of the sheep that used to graze on the very same field that quibbage matches are played on today. Not only was he inspired to write the song "Blue Suede Shoes," which were incidentally ruined in the accident. Not only was he inspired to write a cookbook with several recipes for mutton. He was also inspired to create the popular Witches and Warlock's game we know today as quibbage.

Quibbage matches take place on the front lawn at Hogwashes, about every other week, or more often if the season is rainy. However, if it does rain, matches are canceled and played on the next fair-weather day.

A giant head is positioned at each end of the field. Each head has twelve teeth. There are three slingshotters on each team who using a slingshot, fire rubber balls in an attempt to knock the teeth out of their opposing team's giant head. Each tooth knocked out is worth ten points. On each team, one goalkeeper uses a garbage can lid as a shield to block rubber balls fired at his team's teeth. There are three more members to each team, two whackers, and one driver. The driver is the only team member to ride a lawnmower. The rest of the team rides hoverboards. The whackers use power trimmers to cut the grass where the lawnmower can't get. The game is played until the last blade of grass is cut, which immediately ends the contest. The team that cuts the most grass earns five million points.

Every quibbage match is exciting. However, the quibbage match that pitted the Popular Rich Kids against the Nerds was the highlight of each of Harry's school years. There was a special satisfaction in defeating Faco Maldoy's team. This year, Faco was captain for the Popular Rich Kids. Harry had to admit from what he had seen so far, it was the best team they had ever fielded. He had watched them defeat the Athletic Jocks most impressively. And, of course they had beaten the Party Animals, as was expected.

The Nerd team was doing nearly as well. They had trounced the Party Animals, as expected. They had eked out a win out against the Athletic Jocks. So the two teams would meet in the last game of the season, in mid November, to determine bragging rights, in a game that would decide who was best, and who was second.

That day was today, November 14th. Harry got up early to take care of his John Deere 2000, a bribe from his late Uncle Serious Smack the Clown, and fill it with gas for the match that afternoon. He always took special care to keep it in top condition. Harry is a naturally-gifted driver with five years of playing experience. Ron was in his second year as the Nerd's starting Goalkeeper. For the two of them, their anticipation made the day drag on until the match was ready to begin. Ron has butterflies in his stomach the whole time.

"I don't know how you can stand all this pressure. Before each game, I feel sick to my stomach. I'm so nervous."

"Nonsense, Ron, what you need is something to eat. Something to keep your energy up for the big game," Harry replied.

They went back to their room to get some chocolate slugs. When they returned Enchilada Johnson was giving the rest of the team a few strategic pointers before the match began.

John Madman and Pat Butterball always announced the Hogwashes matches, and today was no exception. John applied the Resounderous spell to his throat, then began to address the crowd.

"Good afternoon, wizards and witches, and welcome to beautiful Hogwashes Field. It's a crisp golden autumn day, perfect conditions for today's match between the Popular Rich Kids…" He paused as a wave of applause and shouting ensued. Then he continued, "who have had a largely successful history versus the Nerd House…" He paused again but this time to an awkward silence. He jumped in again, "since they first met over fifty years ago on this very field. Lately, however, the Nerds seem to have gotten the better of the PRKs, having won the House Cup the last five years in a row. A feat that you'd have to have been around in the 1970's to remember the last time that happened. A win this year would make it an unprecedented six in a row."

"Most attribute their recent success to the play of their sixth year driver, Harry Putter, his John Deere 2000, and his uncanny ability to cheat. I've watched him in all of his matches, and I haven't figured out how he does it, but the stats speak for themselves. He's got the highest driver rating of any driver in history. So, just how does he do it? Well, let's roll the videotape.

On the fields scoreboard big-screen the clip began. There was a life-sized cardboard cutout of Harry Putter. A super-imposed set of lips said in a squeaky elven voice, "I cheated in every one of my quibbage matches to date. Cheating comes as natural to me as to a cheetah. In fact, if I didn't cheat, I wouldn't want to even play. While the other players practice, I practice cheating. I cheat as often as Ron Cheesley cheats on his tests. He's always copying off of Hermione." The crowd booed and jeered. Ron was shocked. How could Harry sell him out so easily?

"We'll be right back, when we return, we'll hear the Hogwashes School Anthem, right after this." When the camera turned off,

Madman pointed his wand at his throat and said, "Muffelous." Then he turned to Butterball and said, "Pat, you're awfully quiet today, you feeling alright?"

"Just great, John, you were going on and on, and I just didn't want to interrupt you," Butterball explained. Then he turned to the gopher and asked, "Can I get some water over here?"

Madman reapplied the Resounderous spell, and readied himself for the camera. "Wizards and witches please join the Hogwashes Choir in the singing of the Hogwashes School Anthem."

Lavatory Brown stepped forward and the crowd hushed. She began singing, and her fellow students joined her a moment later in song:

> Our school is the finest
> Our students the brightest
> Even our evil geniuses are the best.
> None can compare, from the robes that we wear,
> to the fashionable way that we style our hair.
> Hogwashes, Hogwashes, Hogwashes.
>
> Our leader is the finest,
> Our lightbulbs are the brightest,
> Even our G.O.A.T. scores are the best.
> No one can compare, no one even dare,
> if they're too stupid to care, they'd better beware,
> 'cause we'll steal their lunch money at recess.
> Hogwashes, Hogwashes, Hogwashes.
>
> Our food is the finest,
> Our smiles the brightest,
> Send help, we're being held against our will.
> None can compare, don't sit there and stare.
> We need help, call 911, there's no time to spare.

Were trapped at
Hogwashes, Hogwashes, Hogwashes.

Cheers and cries of help rang out at the end of the song.

Madman applied the Resounderous Spell to his throat and began again, "It always moves me to hear the Hogwashes Anthem sung so beautifully. But I think they changed some of the words? Did you notice anything different, Pat?"

Pat applied the Resounderous Spell to himself and replied, "I wasn't listening, John," then he returned to the magazine he was reading, Warlock's Wardrobe.

John took over excitedly, "And here come the Popular Rich Kids' team lead by their captain, Faco Maldoy." The crowd went wild, cheering, screaming, whistling, and stomping their feet.

"Is there anyone who doesn't like the Popular Rich Kids this year? I mean come on, Faco Maldoy is soooo cute." A few of the girls screamed.

"And I've got to think this is their year, what with their new hoverboards, slingshots, robes, and lawnmower, the John Deere 2004! That is one sweet ride-on, huh, Pat?"

Butterball shrugged, "I guess."

Madman gave Butterball a perplexed look, but took over again, "I heard that baby not only cuts the grass, but mulches the clippings! And here come the Nerds, led by their captain, Enchilada what's her face. I have to say, doesn't the Nerds team look more pathetic with each team they field over the years?"

He glanced at Butterball, who turned another page in the magazine he was reading. John didn't pause long for Pat, "But don't be fooled, that twerp, Putter, he may look like a geek, but he sure can cheat! Now, if you direct your attention to the center of the field, today's referee, Ms. Smooch, will conduct today's elf toss!"

Ms. Smooch called out, "As Nerd Team Captain, you get to call the toss. Heads or tails?"

Enchilada Johnson said, "Tails, no Heads! HEADS!"

Ms. Smooch threw the elf up so that it flipped repeatedly in the air, and landed with a thud on its head, then somersaulted a few times until it came to a rest face in the dirt. "Tails, it is!" She turned to Faco Maldoy and asked, "Which goal will you take?"

"That one." Faco indicated the West goal head that his team would defend. The one with the sun behind it, where it wouldn't shine directly into the goalkeeper's eyes mercilessly like the one left for Cheesley to defend.

The teams got into position as Madman introduced the players to the crowd.

The two drivers Faco and Harry revved their engines as Ms. Smooch shouted, "Ready ... Set ...," Faco hit the throttle and took off like a shot, "GO!" Harry coughed a bit at the cloud of dust raised by Faco's John Deere 2004, then took off himself.

"And they're off! Faco takes an early lead on Putter by executing a Premature Departure maneuver to perfection. Meanwhile the Nerd Whackers, Seymour Butz and Tabithaa Stevens, head to the left side of the field to trim the sidewalk."

"And the Popular Rich Kids take an early lead as their slingshotters knock out the first tooth of the game. Second year goalkeeper Cheesely's looking overwhelmed by the combined onslaught of the opposing Slingshotters, Darth Vader, Bobby the elf, and Satan. That was Bobby with the score."

The Poplar Rich Kids in the stands broke into song:

> Cheesley is goof.
> He cannot block a single tooth,
> we're telling you the gospel truth,
> Cheesley is a goof.

Madman's voice boomed over the singing, "On the South side of the field the PRK Whackers Shabby and Foil are trimming around the scattered trees, rocks, and shrubs. And at that goal head, Panties Pimpleton is holding off the Nerd slingshotters, Enchilada what's her face, Ginny Cheesley, and Colin Creepy. Colin Creepy looks particularly inept with his slingshot. What a wimp."

"Looks like more pressure on Cheesley as the PRK slingshotters bombard him. That Satan, boy, can he bring the heat! Ohh! Cheesley took a painful shot to his nose, leaving an opening for Vader, and he scores! It's 20-0 for the PR Kids."

> Cheesley is a clumsy clot,
> he trips over his own feet a lot,
> In a hundred years he won't block a shot,
> Cheesley is a clot.

"Faco cuts Putter off zooming by on his John Deere 2004. Putter swerves to avoid the collision. Faco's cutting a lot of grass, he's really improved on his Driver Efficiency Rating this year. I also like the look of the pattern he's cutting into the grass. Wait what's that? He's writing something out on the North lawn. 'Harry ….Putter….Stinks!' Oh, that's funny! Here comes Putter to erase it with his mower. It's going to take Putter a while to get rid of that."

"Time out, Nerds. Captain Enchilada what's her face doesn't like what's she's seen so far, and she's called time out to rally her team. Stay tuned after these words from our sponsors."

Madman applied the Muffelous spell to his throat, and then asked Butterball for some of his water. "Pat, what's up, you haven't said a thing yet about the game! Aren't you going to help with the commentary?"

"Well, yeah, John. That's why I'm here after all. How about if you let me start off when the game resumes?"

"That would be great."

Meanwhile, Enchilada Johnson started shouting over the noise of the lawnmowers, getting on Ron's case. "We need you to double your efforts Ron! We're falling behind too quickly. I don't know how we're going to catch up!"

Colin Creepy shouted, "Yeah, and I don't like to lose."

Ron's brow was dripping with sweat and already he looked exhausted. He glared at the wimp Creepy with a look of fury. He was already giving everything he could, and really was doing as much as was humanly possible, having made several incredible saves. Creepy on the other had done nothing to score any points for the Nerds, and barely seemed to understand how to use a slingshot. Ron yelled, "Right!" and steeled himself to do even more when the game resumed.

Meanwhile, the Popular Rich Kids were giving each other high fives. Satan was the first to take his shirt off and was flexing and posing. A few of the others soon followed.

Pat Butterball applied the Resounderous spell to his throat then said, "And here we go," as the game resumed. He immediately applied the Muffelous spell, made himself comfortable, and closed his eyes as though ready for a siesta.

Madman almost choked on the water he was drinking, but quickly recovered. "I just thought I'd mention that time outs don't apply to drivers. Drivers would have to be insane to stop cutting. Unless they have some kind of mechanical failure, you want your driver out there cutting grass. Basically, you stop, you lose. The stats prove it. Eleven outta the past twelve times, when the driver stops, whatever the reason, that team loses the match."

"The Nerd Whackers, Butz and Stevens, continue to edge the sidewalk, while the Nerd Slingshotters, Enchilada what's her face, Ginny Cheesley, and Colin Creepy latest inept attempts are thwarted by Pimpleton. They just don't seem to have practiced coordinating their attacks."

At the other end of the field, especially loud banging could be heard as Ron garbage can lid was being pounded by shot after shot from combined onslaught of Satan, Bobby, and Vader, as they began using steel shot instead of rubberballs. Ron had even taken a shot that cracked one of his ribs, but continued to block every piece of steel hurled his way. Several ricochets had even punched holes into the giant head.

Madman continued, "It looks like the PKR slingshotters have doubled their assault on Cheesley. Just look at the dents in his garbage can lid! One can't help but admire their ingenuity substituting steel shot for rubber balls. It's so obvious when they cheat, yet I've been watching Putter, and still haven't seen him cheat, though undoubtedly he must be. Well, maybe this will even things out."

"Maldoy and Putter are really going at it now. They are neck and neck and kicking at each other and each other's mowers as they circle round the field."

"Meanwhile, Seymour Butz and Tabithaa Stevens have moved on to the South side of the field and are competing with Shabby and Foil for trees, rocks, and shrubs to trim. Looks like they are quickly running out of places to trim. But that's to be expected when you have four Whackers on the field as good as these guys."

"And it's another goal for the PKR team! Satan gets credit for the score, Vader for the assist."

> Cheesley is totally spastic,
> You'd better do something drastic,
> Nothing is as well known as,
> Cheesley is a spaz.

"Cheesley's arguing with the field judge. Bad move Cheesley! And the ref, Ms. Smooch, gives him the yellow card! Ouch! He better watch himself now, the Nerd's can't afford to loose Cheesley, should he draw the red card."

"Now the ref is examining the PKR Slingshotters' ammo bags. Looks like their steel ammo is well hidden. No penalty cards are issued. And she blows the whistle, the game resumes."

"Putter and Maldoy begin cutting small left-over patches here and there, as the assault on Cheesley begins afresh. You know, I think he's doing a heck of a job out there, Pat." Madman glanced at Butterball, who was snoring loudly. He resumed, "The kid has a high percentage of shots blocked. But when you have that many shots coming at you, a few are bound to get through. And the PKR slingshotters, have almost 600 more shots taken then the Nerds slingshotters."

"The Whackers are done trimming now, and have started to use their trimmers now on each other's quibbage robes! Butz and Foil are holding each other off, but Stevens is really doing a job on Shabby's robe and now she's using her trimmer on Shabby's hoverboard! I've never seen that before."

"On the North side of the field, Pimpleton just threw her garbage can lid at Enchilada what's her face, bounced it off her forehead, BAM, and caught it again. She's down. And Pimpleton didn't miss a beat, blocking both shots from the other two Nerds."

"And Cheesley's taking another pounding on the other end of the field. The PRK team is using rubber ammo again. But they're slinging it at a furious rate. It's hitting Cheesley's shield so rapidly it sounds like an automatic weapon. Vader uses the force to throw the kitchen sink at Cheesley, who ducks, and it's Satan with the score again! And it's 40 to zip, PRK. The Nerd's call another timeout! They need to apply some smelling salt to their captain. Well be right back after this."

Cheesley is a clumsy klutz,
who doesn't have any guts.
No ifs, ands, ors, or buts,
Cheesley is a klutz.

Madman applied the Muffelous spell to his throat, then woke up Butterball. "Pat, what's wrong with you? It seems like you couldn't care less about this match!"

"Well, yeah, John. It's not really even a sport. Grumblesnore's just tricking these kids into cutting the lawn."

"What are you talking about! You're insane! The next thing you'll be telling me is that pro football is fixed."

Meanwhile, the unconscious Enchilada Johnson woke with a start when the smelling salt was applied under her nose, saying, "I want to ride the pony!" Faco was circling them with his lawnmower, making it difficult to hear themselves over the noisy engine. Harry continued to cut grass. Then she saw the scoreboard and started loudly chewing Ron out, "Ron, you dufus! We're going to lose, and it's all your fault! If you don't keep the rest of those teeth up, I'm going to train a goat to replace you!"

Colin Creepy shouted, "Yeah, can't you …."

Ron's furiously started choking Creepy. Butz and Stevens hauled him off. Then they all took their positions as Creepy shouted a long string of obscenities at Ron that would have made a sailor blush.

Meanwhile, the Popular Rich Kids were drinking Buggerbeer and pouring it all over each other in celebration. Satan was laughing like only the devil could. Then they took their places on the field for the game to resume.

"Welcome back," said Madman, "What's her face is back up, and appears to be able to continue. She hasn't done anything so far. Maybe that blow to the head will improve her game."

"I don't know, it seems to me that Maldoy's doing a much better job of cheating today than Putter. But that's the thing, we never actually see Putter cheat. I mean, it looks to me like he's playing fair, but I'm sure he must be tricking me. I think Maldoy might get caught cheating one of these times, but no way is anyone going to catch Putter."

"The Whackers are going at it again, Butz on Foil. Stevens on Shabby. Stevens is really doing a job of Shabby's hoverboard. I don't know what's holding that thing together still, with the weight of Shabby on top of it, you'd think it would have split by now. Well, there you go! Looks like Shabby's done for today!"

"Creepy just shot himself with his slingshot. He's dropped it."

"Butz and Stevens are double teaming Foil. They've got the elastic of his underwear, and are giving him a painful looking wedgie. OOOOF! I wonder if they, yes, they make it an atomic one, as the elastic comes up over Foil's forehead. Umph!"

"Meanwhile Cheesley is under heavy fire again. Let's take another look at some of the acrobatic saves he's made so far today." The big screen showed Ron hopping about like his pants were on fire, as he made numerous blocks in defense of his goal.

"Cheesley's been amazing today, the Nerds are lucky that the score isn't any worse."

"Maldoy and Putter are now circling the field, they're rapidly mowing down the last patches of grass."

"And Bobby scores! He lobbed that one over Cheesley, arcing it just out of his reach. That's a tough shot. You don't know how hard it is to have that kind of finesse with a slingshot. Cheesley looks exhausted. It's fifty to nothing as we head into the homestretch of this match."

Cheesley is a no-good fink,
in Quibbage games he really stinks,
That's what PRKs all think,
Cheesley is a fink.

"Putter and Maldoy are tied right now, and are circling the field. They're looking for the last bit of grass. That last bit of elusive grass. When they find it, the game is instantly over, not only that, but it looks like whoever gets there first is going to win this one. It all comes down to who wants it more."

"Cheesley's being pummeled again."

"Now, this is where Putter really excels, if I owned a Quibbage team, I would want Putter on my team. Not only does he cheat the best, but he has really good vision when it comes to finding the Missed Spot. How often do we get into these situations, almost every time, someone's out there cutting a lawn, and BAM, they miss a spot. Then they have to ride around searching for the Missed Spot."

"In the past, Maldoy's tried to keep close tabs on Putter. He tries to keep with him, and when Putter finds the Missed Spot, Maldoy tries to get there first. Big mistake! It's cost the PRKs several matches. It always amazes me how close these matches can be."

"Looks like Maldoy's learned something though, this time, he's circling around looking for it himself. Who knows he may get lucky."

"Cheesley in the meanwhile has blocked everything the PRK guys have shot at him."

"Putter veers, he's spotted it, the Missed Spot! Maldoy, too! He's heading for it, too. They're coming for it from opposite sides of the field. This is going to be close."

Hermione stood up and ran from her place in the stands. She licked her finger to test the wind direction, then adjusted a porta-john two feet over. She stood and held the door open.

"They are going to get there at just about the same time! I've never seen a match this close! Either one of them could get it!"

"BAMM! That was some collision. Putter went flying one direction, Maldoy the other. OUCH! Putter landed head first on a rock. Maldoy sailed headfirst into one of them, what do call 'em, portable crappers."

Hermione pulled the handle, flushing Faco's head, causing it to abbarate to the Hogwashes cesspool.

Harry's skull was badly fractured and he lay unconscious in a heap next to the rock he had landed on.

"The field judge is going to have a tough time sorting this one out! We'll wait for her call."

All eyes watched the field, even the school nurse, Ms. Pomfrite, and the local paramedics crew from St. Mongo's, there just in case of injury. But, Ms. Smooch couldn't push the two crumpled tractors apart. Their metal had twisted upon each other, catching, keeping the vehicles locked together. She called for Hasbeen to come pull them apart. A moment later, the huge man had pulled the tractor wreck apart, revealing a tiny patch of uncut grass underneath. Tabithaa Stevens casually whacked it with her trimmer, and the Nerds won 5 million to 50. It had been the closest Quibbage match ever.

Pat Butterball asked sarcastically, "Doesn't the lawn look great?"

Tabithaa Stevens was swept from the field on the shoulders of the celebrating Nerds. Geek laughter reigned supreme that day. And the Popular Rich Kids vowed revenge, no way were they going to be shown up by a bunch of wimpy losers and let them get away with it.

Later that night, Gildersneeze Farthard and Hasbeen were casually walking the freshly cut field, enjoying the smell of the cut grass, when they discovered Harry Putter. Harry staggered to the porta-john where he vomited upon sight of the headless body of Faco Maldoy. Gildersneeze saw that Harry's head was grossly misshapen and recalled the events of the early afternoon Quibbage match. He realized Harry's head had been badly fractured. Pulling his wand from his pocket, he pointed it at Harry.

Harry, though it hurt his head immensely protested, "No! NO!"

But, Gildersneeze didn't remember what had happened the last time he had tried to mend a broken bone, and cast the spell the exact same way, deboning Harry's head. Harry's head was like a thick pudding resting on his neck. He tried to make a face at Farthard, but couldn't. He tried to yell at Farthard, but only managed to gurgle out a thick raspberry. He was having a lot of trouble just breathing.

"You're welcome." Farthard replied.

Hasbeen dragged Faco Maldoy's body to the hospital wing. Using his hand to hold his mouth open so he could breathe, Harry followed.

Chapter 11

The Hospital Wing

In the school's hospital wing, Harry was immediately given a bed. Tubes kept his nasal passages open so he could breathe. As he lay with his head on a pillow, like a sack filled with jello, he felt his eyes wobble with each of his heartbeats. It felt like he was on a waterbed. Luckily, he didn't sneeze. If he did, he would have died, and it wouldn't have been pretty. Luckily, he didn't know that; if he did, he would have sneezed. Instead, he lay there wondering where they were keeping all the Cheesecake-Obsessed children, the unfortunate ones who had been incapacitated after having eaten a cheesecake from the Chamber of Cheesecakes. He guessed that the hospital wing was too small to accommodate such a number of beds. There had been six incidents so far, seven, if you included Belch.

He found it hard to relax with Maldoy's headless corpse in the bed opposite him. Mrs. Pomfrite, the school nurse, was taking care of Maldoy, but Harry couldn't lift his head to watch what she was doing, even if he had wanted to. He figured she was embalming Faco, or what was left of him anyway. He wondered why she would take care of the dead when he was still alive, but he remembered the unintelligible gurgling flatulence that came out of his mouth whenever he tried to talk, and decided to just wait his turn.

He imagined Luscious Maldoy at the funeral for his only son. It would have to be a closed casket funeral, Luscious would never see his son's face again, nor would anyone else for that matter. Putter didn't hold any remorse whatsoever for the Maldoy family, they were known Fungus Eaters. He hoped the Ministry arrested Luscious at the funeral.

But at the same time, he felt bad for Faco, who had died a horrible death. There was no dignity in it. It would have been better if Harry and Faco had held a wizard duel to the death. Then Faco would have died with the respect his enemy deserved.

Faco's death also meant Harry's life would become that much more dull. Having a nemesis to plot against gave meaning to many of Harry's days at Hogwashes for the past five years, six if you counted preschool. He also had spent countless hours in paranoia over how to put a stop to Maldoy's own schemes, both real and as Harry imagined them. Yes, he realized, he was going to miss Maldoy. Cripes, how could Hermione be so insensitive?

Then Mrs. Pomfrite approached with the large bottle labeled "Numbskull Potion" and asked, "So are you ticklish, Mr. Putter?"

He remembered the last time when he had to regrow his right humerus. It had hurt a lot. He was in pain all night as the bone of his arm regrew. So why was she asking if he was ticklish this time? Confused, he tentatively replied, "A little." Unfortunately, it sounded more like an extended burp.

"That's good," she explained, "this new 'Numbskull Potion' rather tickles. And it can be very bad if you are so ticklish that you move a round while your skull is regrowing. So do try to hold still tonight. Try to sleep, if you can."

She took hold of his lip and stretched his mouth open, a lot further than it would have been possible if he had a jawbone. Then she poured the Numbskull Potion down Harry's throat. She let go, and his lip flapped back into place. His whole head wobbled out of control. Harry wondered about her bedside manner, it seemed a bit lacking. Oddly, the thought seemed funny to him. A chortle rose in his throat but as it escaped it sounded more like a raspberry.

Nurse Pomfrite pulled the curtain closed around Harry's bed, then turned the lights out as she left.

If you were in the hospital wing that night, you wouldn't have gotten much sleep. There was one other student there besides Harry, Justin Flinch-Retchedly. He was a Nerd who had been beaten up by Shabby, Foil, and a few other disappointed Popular Rich Kids. During the fight, Justin's ribs had been cracked. Justin was kept up most of the night, at first with the noises of belches, raspberries, and gurgling, later with strange laughing and giggling, all coming from Harry's bed. Harry was the only one who got any sleep. But even his sleep didn't keep him quiet.

Maldoy complained, "Would you shut up! It's enough to wake the dead." He rolled over and covered his new head with a pillow.

Later that night, Harry could be heard eerily droning ingredients and their measures. One and a half cups of sugar, three eggs, one teaspoon vanilla, 32 ounces cream cheese, 1 cup sour cream. Justin Flinch-Retchedly and Faco continued to be kept awake by it at first. However, panic ensued among them when they realized the ingredients all belonged in cheesecake! They fled the hospital wing in great haste.

Word spread very quickly throughout the school in the wee hours of the night. Harry Putter is the Err of Slipperin!

Harry woke the next morning feeling greatly refreshed and very happy, like he had just been to the movies to see his favorite comedy, Rocky III. He yawned. Mrs. Pomfrite walked in to the hospital wing and was greatly alarmed to see the empty beds. Where were her patients? Checking on Harry, she drew the curtain around his bed away.

"Oh, dear!"

"What?" asked Harry, stretching.

"Let's just say, apparently you are a bit more ticklish than you let on," she replied.

"Huh?"

She got a hand mirror out of the drawer and handed it to him. She immediately began to fill a syringe, but he wasn't paying attention to that, in his eagerness to examine his face in the mirror.

"Wow! I look ridiculous!" he laughed. "Good thing you'll be able to straighten it out! Heh, heh, right?"

She administered the shot quickly, and just in time. As she shook her head no, in reply to his question, his scream of anxiety quickly dwindled to a whimper as he passed out from the sedative she had injected.

When Harry woke again, it was dark in the hospital wing. Bobby the elf was sitting on the edge of the bed, holding a deformed ape skull. Harry felt maddeningly ticklish all over for just a second, then the feeling faded away.

"Hi, Bobby, what have you got there?"

Bobby held the strangely grotesque skull up and made the jaw move with his hand as he talked, like a ventriloquist. "Hello Mr. Putter, Sir! I'm your second skull, Sir! Your third one seems to be doing much better."

Harry gave a short laugh. "I'm very thirsty, Bobby, would you get me a glass of water?"

Bobby's eyes widened, "Oh, no, Sir, not water! Bobby mustn't go near water!"

"Huh? Why not?"

"Water is very bad for an elf. Never get water on an elf, Sir! They become terrible, nasty, and dangerously fierce! Wild and uncontrollable, Sir!"

"Calm down, I can get my own water." Harry rolled his eyes. "And people think I'm the drama queen," he thought as he got up and went to the sink.

"Bobby came to visit Harry Putter. Bobby feels just terrible. Harry Putter is in great danger and is very lucky to be alive. When you are better, you must leave school before it is too late."

It was obvious to Harry that Bobby was trying to get him to leave the safety of Hogwashes, and go home where he would be in the reach of his enemies. Obviously, this was Bobby's original plan.

Harry finished drinking, threw his cup in the wastebasket, wiped his mouth on his sleeve, and said, "Bobby, that crash was just an accident."

"Oh, no sir! That accident happened quite on purpose, Sir. Someone cut the brake wire on your tractor!"

"Get out!" Harry gave Bobby a shove that sent him tumbling off the edge of the bed. "Who would do such a thing? Lord Moldyfart?"

"Thank you, Sir! No, Bobby did it. Bad Bobby, BAD Bobby! Please, Sir, hit Bobby again!"

"Stop it, I'm not going to hit you! Someone ordered you to do it, Bobby. Your new master, Lord Moldyfart ordered you, didn't he?"

"Bobby doesn't serve," he paused, "doesn't serve He-Who-Must-Not-Be-Smelled!"

"Who then?"

"Bobby, cannot say. Orders is orders. But master did not say that Bobby couldn't visit Harry Putter, Sir. Bobby came to warn Harry Putter again. Bobby must make Harry Putter understand, next time he won't be so lucky! He must leave Hogwashes!"

"Bobby, I never even tried to use my brakes."

"Oh?....Well then, Bobby never cut them." The elf indignantly walked out of the hospital wing with his nose in the air.

Chapter 12

The Heir of the Err

"Well, if you aren't the Heir of the Err, then why do you suppose you were reciting cheesecake recipes in your sleep?"

"For the last time, Ron, I don't know! I've never made a cheesecake in my life and while I may know some of the ingredients that are in cheesecake, any moron does, you know, I don't know ALL of the ingredients in cheesecake, and I certainly don't know what their measures would be. I think I was channeling. I think Lord Moldyfart was making a cheesecake, and I channeled him while he was doing it."

Many students nearby overheard Harry, as he was getting a bit loud in his exasperation. Several of them bowed down in benediction at the use of the Fart Lord's name.

Ron tried to figure out if he knew any of the ingredients in cheesecake. He felt like a moron for a minute, until he remembered that cheesecake must have cheese in it. He wondered what kind was used in cheesecake, provolone? Parmesan? Ooh, probably Ricotta!

Ron had asked Harry the same question the day Harry had gotten out of the hospital wing, and he was still asking it today, over a month later. It was mid December, the ceiling in the Great Eatery showed that yesterday, even though the sun was out, the sky was gray. The large room was a bit chilly. Grumblesnore, being the tightwad that he is, wouldn't properly heat the school. Students wore thick sweaters to compensate.

History of Magic class was as boring as ever. It wasn't that it didn't have potential for excitement. It was Professor Binge's presentation that made it Harry's most boring class. Hermione seemed to be the only one interested in what Binge had to say. Consequently, she racked up a lot of house cup points by answering his questions right. She was the only one who ever bothered to raise her hand. Binge didn't seem to mind.

Transmogrification was always good. Harry was one of Professor McGooglesnot's favorite students, and she tended to treat him special. He also seemed to have a bit of talent for the subject. McGooglesnot was an excellent teacher, and always kept the student on their toes. They were already transforming vegetables into hamburgers. Which is a very useful talent to know, especially if you don't like vegetables.

Hermione also managed to earn a lot of house cup points in Transmogrification. McGooglesnot showed favoritism toward the Nerds. Harry figured it only balanced out the points that Professor Ape subtracted from them.

However, it was most shocking when Professor McGooglesnot disappeared suddenly and without a trace. She simple didn't show up for breakfast one morning, which was very unlike her. Her office and rooms were searched. A general search of the school grounds was also conducted, but no evidence of an altercation or abduction were found, nor any note to explain her sudden disappearance. Rumors began circulating that she had been kidnapped and was being held captive in the Chamber of Cheesecakes by a dreadful monster.

Grumblesnore hired a hideous substitute hag, Emphysema Blacklung, to teach Transmogrification until Professor McGooglesnot hopefully returned. Suddenly, Transmogrification class was no longer comfortable. Emphysema had a different way to do everything. She was almost as ugly as Gretchen Shoemacher. Harry found the whole situation to be an added incentive to locating the Chamber of Cheesecakes. The sooner he did, the sooner he could save McGooglesnot, and the sooner Emphysema Blacklung would be out of his life. Surprisingly enough, Hermione's daily accumulation of house cup points increased when Blacklung took over.

In Defense Against the Fine Arts, Professor Farthard continued to subject the sixth year students in Harry's class to more and more deadly creatures. It was becoming a regular thing to see injured or slain students taken to the hospital wing during class. Mrs. Pomfrite complained loudly. Was she expected to work miracles? However, the students were fascinated by Professor Farthard, and greatly anticipated his class. Even those who were killed generally looked forward to the next dangerous encounter. Harry, Ron, and Hermione worked together in class, and though hard pressed at times, managed to avoid being maimed or killed.

The centaur Frenzy continued to reprimand the human race in Astro-Numerology. The students that marveled at the magnificence of the centaurs did well in class. Those who attempted to argue on behalf of their race suffered poor marks. Harry found it very easy to kiss up to the centaur. He got an A on his report, "Why I wish I were a centaur," even though he wished no such thing.

In Magical Beast Biology, Professor Hasbeen was teaching them about Groundysnouts. Groundysnouts were swine with wings, and were usually seen after someone used the cliché, "when pigs fly." They were also very delicious if one could manage to catch one, which was seldom.

In "Sawing" class, Humphrey the Wise and Mystical was explaining the classic, How to pull a Rabbit out of a Hat.

In Poisons class, Carnivorous Ape continued to dock house cup points from Harry for not having his cauldron. Harry was also failing. He couldn't do any of the work without his cauldron.

After Poisons, Harry continued to study yoga with Ape. Most of the time, Harry was trying to achieve "inner peace." However, the mere mention of "inner peace" made him fidgety.

Quibbage season was over, and there were no practices to attend. Ron had collapsed under Hermione's steady pressure; he joined the OSPREE club. He remained constantly on the lookout for any excuse to get out of OSPREE meetings. Harry continued to decline to join, leaving no uncertain terms. He claimed that with the added burden of "Remedial Poisons" with Professor Ape, that he was already overburdened.

The attempts on Harry's life were becoming few and far between. He had survived too many attempts on his life for his fellow students to believe that he was killable. Many had driven a knife into his back with their own hands, only to see him eating as usually in the Great Eatery the next morning. Rumors that he was immortal were circulating. Someone had even driven a wooden stake into the dummy's heart, in case Harry was a vampire. Many had given up. If He-Who-Must-Not-Be-Smelled couldn't kill Harry, then who could?

Meanwhile, there had also been a rather unsettling incident the week before. It seemed that Ophelia Quirkey, a fellow sixth year Nerd, had gotten it in her head that Hermione being the nerdiest of all the Nerds was not worthy of Ronald Cheesley's affections. After all, what did Hermione Stranger have that she didn't, besides an overly large head. She felt she was a much more suitable girlfriend for Ron, and she decided to let Ron know it. She started flirting with him. After two days of it, Hermione couldn't take it any more.

She told Ophelia to keep her hands and eyes "off her man!" Ophelia told Hermione that she didn't deserve a man, if she didn't know how to take care of one. That's when the fight started, or perhaps more exact, the beating started. Hermione fought mean. It eventually took two teachers, Smooch and Tickwick, to finally pull her off from Quirkey. Thereafter, the flirting stopped. Harry couldn't believe it, girls were actually fighting over Ron, while he couldn't even get up the nerve to talk to Yu Rang. She seemed so unapproachable before she had a boyfriend. Now that she was seeing Michael Coronary, it was a total impossibility.

Even more disturbing, there had been three more cheesecake incidents since Harry had gotten out of the hospital wing. Bringing the total of the Cheesecake Obsessed to nine, ten if you included Belch. Those who were laid up in the hospital wing, or probably somewhere nearby, were: Todd Oreobreath, Henrietta Widowmaker, Bonibal Snowman, Valiant Effort, Goerthe Von Goop, Ignatius "Iggy" Zweebler, Formalda Hyde, Woody Sawdust, and Aloyicius Mudhead. Most of them were Popular Rich Kids. However, Iggy was a Party Animal, Valiant Effort was a Jock, and Aloyicius Mudhead was a Nerd. The only thing they all had in common was that Harry didn't know any of them, not even his fellow Nerd, Mudhead. Harry blamed himself. If only he were more social, he might get to know more of the other students.

Grumblesnore had seemingly done nothing to locate and close the Chamber of Cheesecakes. Harry hadn't exactly been following Grumblesnore's command to leave the mystery alone.

Harry had already searched both the Locker Room and the Party Animal's Common Room, but hadn't found any recipe books at all. He had also searched many private rooms only to come up empty. He had focused on the rooms of preschoolers figuring that the Heir to the Err had to be someone new to the school, or else the Chamber of Cheesecakes would have opened sooner. He searched Farthard's chamber, too, for the same reason. However, he couldn't even find a recipe book, not even in the school kitchen.

During his searches, he had several close encounters with Professor Ape. Ape appeared to be after Putter, roaming the corridors late at night. There was little doubt, Ape had it in for Putter, and wanted to see him expelled. Putter had thus far managed to elude him.

They had made no progress on solving the mystery. In fact, if anything they were more confused than ever. Soon the holiday break would be here. All of the other students would be going home for the holidays, their families wanted to see them. Harry was the only one who remained at school this time of year. He looked forward to using the time to conduct a thorough search for the cheesecake recipe book.

People were still pointing at Harry and whispering, just like his first day back from the hospital wing. Hermione said, "Just ignore them," as she read People magazine. She seemed to ignore an elf that without her permission crept up and began polishing her cauldron. It was another one of the elves methods, if they could somehow serve unnoticed, the human might grow accustomed to their service, and it might grow on them. A moment later, –Wham! Hermione wholloped the elf with a fly swatter she carried just for that purpose. Harry was becoming worried about Hermione's violent nature. He found it unsettling. Getting into fights, swatting elves, killing Maldoy, what was next? He attributed it to books. After all, she didn't listen to violent lyrics in rock songs, watch movies or television, and since human beings are not violent by nature, what else could it be? However, he was too scared to confront her over it. She might hurt him.

Ron just kept wondering if Harry really was the Err of Slipperin. He was very skeptical of Harry's answer. He asked, "But why would Lord …" He quieted his voice to a whisper, "He-Who-Must-Not-Be-Smelled be baking cheesecake? Doesn't he have better things to do with his time? You know, like plotting your death and torturing kittens and stuff?"

"Heck, Ron, even Fart Lords have gotta eat, and who doesn't like cheesecake?"

Ron sighed unconvinced. He toyed with the wand he had broken a few minutes earlier. He had sat on it by mistake.

Hermione continued reading, unconvinced.

Harry too was unconvinced. He thought to himself, "Am I the Err of Slipperin?" Somehow, he had to find out. Then it hit him. It was time to pay a little visit to the biggest blabbermouth on Hogwashes, and get him to do some serious gut spilling.

So he cut History of Magic class, and headed to Hasbeen's log cabin on the edge of the Forbidden Forest of Sure Death. He knocked on Hasbeen's door.

"Who be there?" replied the fattest man at Hogwashes, while Harry wondered why he hadn't done this sooner.

"It's me, Harry."

" 'arry OOH?"

"Harry Putter, that's who, you big lummox!"

"C'mon in, 'arry."

Harry let himself in. Bicuspid leapt up on Harry and slobbered on his face. "Get down you mangy… umm…I mean, good dog."

Hasbeen was wearing an apron and making a graham cracker crust in the kitchen. "Hi, 'arry. Make yerself comfortable like. 'ow's school goin'? Shouldn't ye be in class?"

"Fine. No, not until ten," Harry lied. "How's things with you? What's new?"

"Nuttin' much. Played Bingo las' night, but that mysterious man weren't there this week. Sit doon and 'ave some tea and errrr …"

Hasbeen threw a towel over some cheesecakes fresh from the oven and cooling on the countertop, "crackers?"

"What mysterious man?"

"The creepy 'ooded man who never tells me 'is name. 'e comes e'ery so often. 'e's the one that gives me all them dogs, Bicuspid, errr Muffy, and Skippy. Oh yeah, and that dragon egg, 'member that? Ahhhh now, that were a bit o' fun."

Harry took a couple of crackers with his tea. He couldn't forget Bicuspid, the stupid dog was right there and wouldn't take his eyes off Harry's crackers. He remembered Muffy the three-headed offspring of Cerberus that had guarded the Sorcerous Stone years ago. He also remembered the baby dragon that Hasbeen had hatched. But, who was Skippy? Was Skippy the poodle? "I don't remember Skippy. What kind of dog was he?"

"The most incredible poodle I've e'er seen. He's a fine guard dog!"

"BINGO," Harry thought. "Where is he?" he asked. He didn't need to look around for the dog. He knew Skippy was in that strange room on the sixth floor guarding the trapdoor.

"Oh, I lent 'er to Grumblesnore to 'elp guard the entrance to the Chamber of Cheesecakes." Hasbeen replied nonchalantly as he finished pouring creamy batter into a pie tin, and put it in the oven.

Harry thought, "So Grumblesnore has known from day one where the entrance to the Chamber of Cheesecakes is. He's keeping curious students out, probably because the Chamber is guarded by some fantastic and dangerous beast. We wouldn't want kids to wander in there, now, would we?"

"So, 'ow, I mean, how do you get past the poodle?"

"Well, I can't tell ya that, I'm sworn to secrecy."

Harry stared at Hasbeen.

A moment later Hasbeen broke. "Oh, all right, I'll tell ya! Ye hast to bring a full grown cow with ya, and while the dog is devour'n the cow, ya runs past, right quick."

"I see.   And do you have any other information about the Chamber of Cheesecakes?"

"Nope! Tha's everything."

Harry stared at Hasbeen. A drop of sweat dripped from the fat man's brow, and he stole a glance over at the pie tins cooling under the towel.

"Well, I guess that really is all you got," said Harry rising from his chair. "Thanks for the tea and crackers."

"Any time, any time."

As Harry climbed the hill from Hasbeen's cabin toward the back door of Hogwashes, Hasbeen let out a sigh of relief.

No, Hasbeen wasn't the Heir of the Err of Slipperin. All the talk of cheesecake going on lately had made him pretty hungry for some. However, there would be no explaining that to some people. "It's a good thing that boy is so oblivious," thought the enormous man.

Chapter 13

The Forbidden Forest
of Sure Death

"A full grown cow?" asked Ron. "Where are we going to get a full grown cow? Are you mad?"

"Have you any idea how expensive an entire cow is?" Hermione balked. "We don't have that kind of cash! We'll have no choice but to steal one."

Harry stared at Hermione agape, "I think we've become a bad influence on you, Ms. Perfect."

"Well, we don't!" she said with exasperation.

"Of course we'll steal one. I'm just surprised to hear you suggesting it is all. You're usually, well, a little uptight about such things." He affected a terrible cowboy drawl, "Cattle-rustlin's a hangin' offense in these here parts, Ma'am."

"All right, so we have no choice but to steal one, where the heck are we going to find a cow to steal around here? Are you mad?" asked Ron.

"Hey, I got an idea. Ron, why don't you stay here at school for the holidays, and we'll conduct a thorough search of the whole school for the recipe book, while Hermione figures out how to get a cow?"

Ron objected, "And miss Christmas? You are mad!"

Hermione objected, "You're putting this whole cow thing on me?"

Ron added, "Look, Harry, if you want to come home with me to the Boil, you're welcome to, but I'm not staying here for Christmas. Only a loser would stick around here." Ron used his wand as if it were a drumstick, "Ba Bump Ba, Ching!"

Harry gave him a look that said, "You're not funny," as Ron whacked the table with his wand and promptly broke it.

"Now THAT's funny!" Harry laughed at Ron's miserable turn of events.

Hermione sighed.

Ron examined his broken wand.

Harry conceded, "All right, I'm sorry. Cripes, I'll stay here and search for the recipe book. You and Hermione try to figure out where we can get a cow."

It never occurred to them to try and find any of the dozens of easier solution to get past the poodle than stealing a cow such as: finding a way to tranquilize the dog, using pepper spray, wearing one of the many suits of armor in Hogwashes to neutralize the dog's teeth, or bringing Hermione's cat, Croakshanks, along. Croakshanks would have easily frightened the poodle.

The next day, all the students would be heading home for the holidays, so three days before Christmas, they exchanged gifts. Hermione gave Ron a framed picture of the two of them, and a garbage can lid. Ron was thrilled with the garbage can lid; his old one had been badly battered during the last quibbage match. She gave Harry a cauldron, so he'd stop losing Nerd House Cup points by being unprepared in Poisons class.

Ron gave both Harry and Hermione socks. His mother had knitted them herself.

Harry gave Hermione an overdue library book. She had taken it out for Harry back in October. Harry had never returned it. She had been nagging him for two months to give it back. She was very happy to receive it.

Harry gave Ron an acoustic guitar.

"Wow! Where did you get it?" asked Ron, impressed.

"Internet," Harry lied.

Harry spent Christmas Eve playing poker with the ghosts. They all warmly congratulated him on the fact that he was still alive and making an exciting show for those who had wagered upon his survival at the beginning of the year. Those who bet against him admitted that they never expected him to last this long.

During the days that followed, Harry conducted an extensive search of Hogwashes. He even searched the girls' bathrooms and Grumblesnore's office. He didn't find any recipe books. Nor during all that time he spent alone wandering the school, did he ever come across a cheesecake vending machine. Harry had a feeling, if he was meant to come across a cheesecake buying opportunity, one would have appeared to him by now.

He spent New Years Eve playing poker with the ghosts while a blizzard blanketed the school grounds in a meter and a half of snow. Hogwashes looked beautiful covered in snow and icicles. Lake Iwannabealifeguard was frozen over. If the other kids were around they could have had a wonderful snowball fight. Instead, Harry spent the next two weeks watching television all day in his underwear, and getting hooked on several ridiculously silly soap operas in the process.

Finally, the students returned. When people asked Harry how his Christmas had been, he replied, "Good." It was much easier than explaining how boring and unfestive the whole time had actually been.

Harry reported to Ron and Hermione there were no recipe books anywhere within Hogwashes. Hermione concluded, "Whoever the Heir of the Err was, he had taken the recipe book home with him for the holidays. The Heir was keeping his secret carefully guarded."

Ron asked, "How do you know it's a he?"

Though she had meant he or she, Hermione sniffed, "Girls are never that stupid."

Ron was very proud to report that he had located a dairy farm approximately twenty-two kilometers away where they could attempt to steal a cow.

"That's nothing," said Hermione. "I located a small farm that's only six kilometers away."

"Six kilometers! Wow, this is going to be easy!" said Harry.

"Not quite, it's on the other side of the Forbidden Forest of Sure Death."

"Well, we can forget about that then," Ron laughed nervously, "right?"

"Actually, no," Hermione replied.

"Crap, I knew you'd want to go to your own farm, instead of mine! Why? Why can't we just this once do things the safe way," spluttered Ron.

"Well, where do you want to go, Ron? The Hogwashes kitchen? They don't even use real beef there. Your farm's twenty-some kilometers from here. We can't walk over twenty kilometers, steal a cow, and get back without being missed. We'll all be expelled."

Harry chimed in, "Yeah, don't be such a COWard, Ron! Get it? COW-ard! We've been to the Forbidden Forest of Sure Death before, and it's not so bad. And I doubt we'll run into any of those nasty giant spiders this time."

"What? I'm not worried about spiders."

Harry and Hermione burst out in laughter.

"Well, I'm not! Maybe I was afraid of the...gulp.... five meter spiders four years ago, but I'm not afraid of 'em anymore."

Hermione pulled out her wand and said "Unga Bunga Bunga Binga Binga Binga Bunga." She waived the wand and a silver-blue light struck the portrait of the two fat ladies at the entrance to the Nerd House. They changed into an enormous portrait of two fat spiders. The spiders seemed eager to get off the canvas and eat them.

Ron backed away with a revolted look on his face.

Harry imitated Ron, "What? I'm not afraid of ... gulp ... spiders."

Ron became furious, "That's it. I'm sick of you two, go find a cow yourselves. I'm not going to risk getting expelled for you two losers!"

Harry apologized, "Sorry, Ron, that was very immature of us." Hermione turned the portrait back to the fat ladies, nodding her head in agreement with what Harry said.

Harry held out his hand and asked, "Friends?"

Ron's ego relaxed with the sincerity of Harry's apology, and he almost grabbed Harry's hand to shake it, but then he saw the tarantula Harry was holding out to him.

"Very funny!" Ron said indignantly and turned to leave. Harry was laughing.

Hermione grabbed Ron's arm. "Oh stop, Ron, with all those brothers and sisters, can't you take a joke? We were just teasing. But seriously, if you aren't afraid of spiders...."

At this Harry started to laugh out of control. She gave Harry a serious look, and it turned out he was able to control his laughter rather quickly.

"If you aren't afraid of spiders, what are you scared of? Werewolves?"

"No!" said Ron with all the indignation he could summon.

"Well, what then?"

"I just don't … want to run into any …"

"Any what?"

"Squirrels."

"Squirrels?" blinked Hermione.

"Yeah, squirrels."

"Well, don't worry about that, Ron, there aren't any squirrels in the Forbidden Forest of Sure Death."

Ron gave Hermione a puzzled look.

"The spiders ate them all," she explained.

It had been the coldest winter Harry could remember. Grumblesnore was too big of a cheapskate to keep the school warm enough in this weather. Students began wearing coats, gloves, and hats to class. The snow on the ground lasted for weeks. Smaller snowfalls had added to the accumulation. Everyone was getting sick of the dreariness outside.

Ron, Harry, and Hermione decided to wait until the spring thaw before they would steal a cow. Hermione said, "It will be bad enough trying to drag a cow through five kilometers of deadly forest without adding snow to the equation." Harry kept praying for an early spring.

They also decided when the time came, to cut Poisons class. They needed to make sure that they got back before it got dark out. The trip would be far less dangerous if they could avoid being in the Forbidden Forest of Sure Death at night. For Harry it was a bonus to miss Poisons class with his least favorite teacher, Ape. Hermione as usually was upset about the idea of missing class, but when Harry pointed out that the Forbidden Forest of Sure Death was also educational, she had to agree. Harry even suggested that she bring a binder and take notes, and it wasn't too long before Hermione was getting excited and packing various other school items for the trip, her objections forgotten.

During this time, Spleen Thomas and Shameonus Finnigan, Harry's and Ron's roommates disappeared without a trace. Like with Professor McGooglesnot's disappearance, it was a total mystery. The same rumors were tossed around explaining the sudden and suspected abductions. Most agreed that they must be captives in the Chamber of Cheesecakes.

During this time, there were also three more of the usual cheesecake attacks. Amber Glow, Moe Money, and Benevolent Dictator were the victims. Harry didn't have a clue who any of them even were. The names seemed oddly familiar, but he couldn't even place a face with the names. That is, until all their faces appeared in the Daily Asylum. Hermione unfolded the paper one morning, and the story was on the front page, including a picture of each of the victims, now thirteen in all. The headline read:

Cheesecake Calamity Strikes Local School, Thirteen Hospitalized, Ministry to Investigate

In addition to what they already knew, the article mentioned that the school was under an investigation that was being conducted by Perky Cheesley. The Ministry was going to get to the bottom of this. It seemed likely this time Grumblesnore would get the axe.

Harry cursed the weather. If only he could get a cow, he knew he could battle the monster in the Chamber of Cheesecakes, destroy the recipe book, and close the sinister chamber forever. He knew he could rescue those who had disappeared, and get the Ministry of Magic off of Grumblesnore's back. He would once again be the hero. He pictured the cheering crowd carrying him on their shoulders, and chanting, "Putter, Putter, Putter!"

Meanwhile, Ron became almost unrecognizable. He seemed to have become rather full of himself ever since the Ophelia Quirkey incident. For some reason, he had adopted the attitude that he was God's gift to women, or at least nerdy adolescent ones. He started treating Hermione like she'd better shape up, if she expected him to keep her around. A week before Valentine's Day, she couldn't stand his inflated ego anymore and told him off. This drove Ron to break up with Hermione, which infuriated her. How could he break it off with her, when she had just told him what an insensitive clod he was, and it was obvious to everyone that wasn't an insensitive clod, that she had broken up with him first.

They began avoiding each other. If Harry was with one, the other would keep their distance, usually Ron ended up sitting alone in the Great Eatery.

Then, the day before Valentine's Day, Ron sat down next to Ophelia Quirkey. They were being a bit too friendly. Hermione couldn't talk to Ron about it. She made Harry find out what was going on.

Harry sadly reported back to Hermione that Ron was indeed seeing Ophelia, and had even asked her to sit next to him on the submarine ride to Atlantis. Hermione was crushed. Ron had never even asked her out officially, –the weasel. Harry felt bad for Hermione, but was secretly pleased. He realized he had been jealous of Ron the whole time he had a girlfriend while Harry didn't.

When Valentines Day arrived, things finally warmed up outside. Love was in the air. While many students were thinking of their sweethearts, Harry was thinking about a cow, that is, stealing a cow. Actually, for an instant he thought about approaching Yu Rang and telling her how much he liked her. The thought made his heart race and a lump form in his throat. No, he just couldn't.

Ginny, however, did not suffer from the same shyness. She pulled Harry aside and pronounced her undying love for him. She said she worshipped the ground he walked on. She told him that she would serve him all her days, if he thought that one day he might feel toward her the smallest portion of the way she felt toward him. He sighed and gave her a sympathetic hug. He thought he was all too familiar with unrequited love.

Hermione feigned nonchalance, hiding her sadness and anger. Harry knew she wanted to scratch Ophelia's eyes out, but any sign of her anger would only make Ophelia and Ron closer. Harry tried all day to distract her.

Two days later, Ophelia dumped Ron. Her friends didn't care for him one bit, and they convinced her that he was a loser and she could do much better. She let Ron down gently, saying that it was the squid.

After a week of warm weather, the grounds outside thawed. Lake Iwannabealifeguard was no longer frozen. Ron made a hard decision. He released Nemoy into the cold water of the lake in back of the school. It was the hardest thing he ever had to do. He shed a single tear when he said a fond goodbye to his playful and ever-faithful pet. Harry was there. He patted Ron's shoulder to comfort his friend.

When Ron informed Ophelia that he had given up Nemoy for her. She wasn't even touched by the act. She confessed, it really was him, not the squid.

Ron was a pitiful sight thereafter, sitting all alone in the Great Eatery. He was too embarrassed to crawl back to Harry and Hermione. So Harry convinced Hermione that they should go to him, and soon they had patched their friendship. Hermione, however, made it quite clear that she didn't accept Ron back as a boyfriend, and she remained emotionally distant with him. When he asked her to sit next to him on the submarine ride to Atlantis, she declined.

She was inwardly thrilled that her plan had worked. Well, not quite as well as she had expected; she hadn't planned on Ron getting hurt in the process. She had figured Ron would be happily in another relationship. But, she knew that Ron would recover, and would be better in the long run for the experience. Maybe she could even help him find another girl friend. In reality, she owed Ron a big thank you. Ron had helped her hook the fish she was really after. All she had to do now was carefully reel him in.

Harry, Ron, and Hermione decided it was time to steal a cow. They cut their Poisons Class and walked out the back entrance to Hogwashes. It was cold outside, cold enough that they could see wisps of water vapor in the air as they breathed out. They walked past the lake, past Hasbeen's cabin, past the Magical Creature Petting Zoo, and into the Forbidden Forest of Sure Death.

The edge of The Forest was much like any forest. The trees were sparse at first, but quickly became more dense. The undergrowth was out of control, and consisted mostly of wild thorn bushes that had to be circumnavigated. The floor was covered with matted down leaves. Here and there were patches of snow in the most shadowy places. They could hear distant primal screams and the crashes of the ferocious creatures, monsters, and nightmarish beasts within.

Harry said, "I think the loud creatures aren't nearly as dangerous as the quiet ones. I mean generally, they're just making all that noise because something silent but deadly lethal just sunk its fangs into them."

Hermione nodded, "And don't forget to watch for quicksand!"

Ron stuck his fingers in his ears, and said, "La, La, La, La." He wasn't dealing with the situation very well.

Harry led the way, stumbling over a root as he pulled his robe hem free from a sticker bush. The sun cast shadows of branches on the leaf-covered floor of the forest hundreds of feet below. Harry lead the group around a feral pack of Cheshire kittens that was tearing the carcass of a mouse apart, while Hermione jammed her wand into the eye of a seal pup to drive it off, all while Ron narrowly avoided being ensnared in the coils of a garden snake by shear dumb luck.

A moment later, Harry drove off a flock of deadly free-range chickens by imitating the call of their most fearsome predator, the chickenhawk. Meanwhile, Hermione spotted a small but ferocious herd of deer, and didn't hesitate to drive spell after spell at the savage hoofed creatures. She knew it was kill or be killed. Ron all the while, bought cookies from each Girl Scout he met in order to assuage their angry wrath.

Before Harry knew it, he was backing away from a huge monstrous insect the likes of which he had never seen before. He knew he'd have nightmares about it the rest of his life. Hermione yelped as a patch of mud sucked at her shoe nearly pulling it off. She shuddered to think about what a close call that had been. If there had been any more mud, it could have taken her right shoe clean off! Ron meanwhile, had a problem of his own. A wiener dog had picked up their scent and was trailing them despite all his efforts to shoo it away. It's yip-like bark, lolling tongue, and waggling tail all signs of imminent attack, Ron thought. "Don't Panic, Ron!" He was on the verge of hysteria, then, inspiration struck! He picked up a stick and threw it as far as he could. The wiener dog shot like a bolt! Ron wiped the perspiration from his brow. Then he wondered why the dog went in a complete different direction than the stick.

The next thing he knew, they were completely surrounded by Arglebarg the ten meter tall spider chief and at least two dozen of her gargantuan children along with hundreds of her grandchildren, much smaller, but still huge by any spider standards. The spiders had dropped down from the canopy of spider webs and leaves above instantly surrounding their prey, Ron, Harry, and Hermione.

Harry noticed there were several bundled up people hanging in the trees above too. The spiders had ensnared them and tied them tight in their webs to eat later. Harry pointed up and said, "Look there's Hootie and the Blowfish!"

Hermione and Ron looked up too and began to point out others.

"And oh my God! That's Adam Sandler!" pointed Hermione.

"There's Marilyn Manson!" pointed Ron.

"I see that guy from Baywatch, what's his name again, David Hasselback?" Harry asked.

"Hasselstein," corrected Ron incorrectly.

"You guys watch too much TV, oh my God! Look up there, there's Michelle Geller!" Hermione pointed.

"Where?" asked Ron. She pointed until Ron could see her.

Harry asked, "Is that Will Young?"

Ron said, "Yeah, but I don't know who those old guys are next to him."

"I think that's the Rolling Stones," said Hermione, "but it might be Jefferson Starship or something. Who knows?"

"I see Keira Knightley," pointed Harry.

"And there's Tom Cruise," said Ron.

"I just love gazing at the stars!" sighed Hermione.

"Hey, what's with the thirteen dwarves up there? What are they from?" asked Ron.

"Beat's me," shrugged Harry.

"Hey, isn't that the Ford Anglia Ice Cream Van that helped you get away from those ugly spiders like four years ago?" asked Hermione.

"Yeah, looks like they got her in the end," replied Ron with a sigh.

"Ahem!" interrupted Arglebarg angrily.

Harry turned his head and noticed the spider chief again. "Uh, guys? We forgot about the spiders." Ron and Hermione were quickly brought back to the reality of their situation.

"I'm glad you like our collection, would you care to get a closer look?" asked the monstrous spider hungrily. Hundreds of spiders started to close in on their prey, even though the three children were barely a snack for some of the largest ones.

"Wait!" shouted Hermione. The spiders paused.

"What is it, child?" asked Arglebarg who had a bit more patience than the younger spiders.

"Errr, …. Hasbeen gave us a message to give to you," Hermione lied. Hasbeen was the one responsible for raising the giant spider, Arglebarg, and Arglebarg was responsible for all the other abnormally large spiders in The Forest. They were all her children.

"A message from Hasbeen? What is his message?" asked Arglebarg, remembering the friend who raised her as a child, feeding her delicious bunnies, kittens, rats, and such.

"Hasbeen says, errrrr," thought Hermione.

"Yes? Yes?" implored the chief spider.

Harry jumped in as Hermione struggled, "Hasbeen says that he wants to invite you all to a reunion party!"

"A reunion party?" Tears were forming in the eight eyes of Arglebarg.

"Yes," said Hermione.

"But how will Hasbeen feed all of us?" the giant spider asked eagerly. "There are not enough rats, bunnies, and kittens in all of Hogwashes. There aren't even enough elves to feed us all. That's why Hasbeen let me go into The Forest in the first place."

"Errrrr, ummmm, Harry?" Hermione came up blank again.

Harry jumped in again, "Hasbeen's going to feed you the students at Hogwashes. He's going to feed you the Popular Rich and very Tasty Kids."

Arglebarg began to drool at the thought. "This is too good to be true! When is the party?"

Harry continued to answer the chief's questions, "Friday the 13th at 3pm, and don't forget to bring your appetite."

"Aah, yes, we wouldn't miss it for the world!" the ten-meter monster replied happily.

"And how many guests should Hasbeen expect then?" asked Harry.

"All of us, that's me, my twenty eight children, and two hundred and eighty six grandchildren. Three hundred fifteen of us in all."

Harry, Ron, and Hermione began to feel like they might just get out of this alive yet.

"Right then, so we'll just let Hasbeen know you'll be coming," said Harry as his friends and he began backing away.

"Where do you think you are going children?"

"Well, we do have to tell Hasbeen you are coming, after all!" replied Harry coolly.

"It only takes one of you to do that!" laughed Arglebarg fiendishly. The spiders began creeping forward. Ron screamed a high-pitched shriek, that Harry thought sounded more like a girl screaming. Then all of a sudden, a squirrel appeared out of nowhere making three quick chomps on one of Arglebarg's eight legs. She howled with pain and rage. The same squirrel seemed to be everywhere at once, throwing acorns at one spider, jumping on another, biting a third. It wove through their legs and pounced on them with blinding speed. Spiders began clunking their heads together, and wrapping each other up in webs aimed at where the squirrel had been just a moment before. Eight eyes were not enough for any spider to keep track of the squirrel as it weaved in and out of their brothers and sisters wreaking havoc. Soon the spiders were in chaos shouting in their despair as the squirrel simply ran circles around them, biting and scratching.

"Now's our chance," Harry yelled, hoping that Hermione and Ron would hear him over Ron's piercing and unending scream, and the three friends took off at a run leaving the squirrel to battle three hundred and fifteen giant spiders. Ron was still screaming as he ran.

Grub the Giant, Hasbeen's half brother, winced as the much too loud scream blasted his ears much like a shrieking siren of an ambulance, as they flew by him. They ran past centaurs and werewolves who were too stunned by the sudden screaming appearance and disappearance of the three students, to react. They ran past confused bugbears and bandersnatches that looked up at the sudden high-pitched noise, but were unable to bring their eyes into focus on the creature or creatures that flew by suddenly while making it. They frightened bogarts and banshees as the high-pitched scream of Ron's was suddenly wailing in the spooks' ears, then gone as quickly as it had come.

Then the three stopped running when they came to a mansion, deeper than they had ever been in The Forbidden Forest of Sure Death. They panted trying to catch their breath.

"What is this place?" Hermione voiced the question on all of their minds.

The mansion grounds were surrounded by a six-foot tall wrought-iron fence. Through the fence they could see the huge white classical building. From their angle they could also see a distant tennis court and swimming pool in a gardenlike backyard. About a half a kilometer behind, cattle were in a corral next to a stucco ranch building. More of The Forest was beyond the clearing surrounding the mansion and its grounds.

"Those are cows!" said Ron blinking to make sure they were real.

Ron walked down to the front gate, and opened it. He called, "It's open, should we go inside?"

As Harry approached he noticed a seal on the gate. It was a shield-like crest with a cheesecake in the center. Harry gaped at it for a moment, pointing at it for the others to see, "Hummmina, Hummina, Hmmmmmmm."

He said, "You two get a cow, I'm going to go inside and see if I can get some answers. I'll bet we'll soon know who the Err of the Heir really is!"

"Forget it, Harry, I'm going too," said Hermione, her curiosity would not allow her to keep away.

"What? You guys aren't going in there, are you? What if there's squirrels inside?" said Ron with a note of panic in his voice.

"Are you kidding, Ron?" asked Hermione incredulously. "That squirrel just saved your life!"

"No way! It was eating those spiders alive, and we were going to be dessert!"

"Well, I guess you can stay here and keep a look out for us," said Harry.

Ever the chicken, Ron said, "Heh, heh, on second thought, I think I'll come too."

They pulled out their wands and walked up the path that led from the gate to the front steps of the mansion. They walked between massive classical pillars supporting a huge pediment above them. Harry looked in the windows next to the door. The front hall had a huge marble staircase curving upward to a landing with some huge windows, there was the same cheesecake crest carved into the floor of the hallway, with a huge crystal chandelier above. No one was in sight.

Ron knocked on the door.

"Ron, you idiot! Why did you knock?" Harry was furious.

"What? Don't we want to see who's home?"

"No, you twit! What an ignoramus! How could I be so stupid as to bring YOU along to steal a cow! Why don't you just phone the police now, and turn us in? I can't believe what a clod you are! What are you going to say when someone answers the door, Ron? 'Ummm, hello, we're here to take a cow, can we borrow a rope to lead it away?' Oh, why? Why, do I have to put up with such a dork? What an IDIOT!" ranted Harry.

Hermione held her fingers to her lips and whispered, "Shhhh, Harry, your shouting just made far more noise than Ron did by knocking, and if anyone's listening, you just told them what we're doing here. Very stupid, indeed!"

But no one answered the door.

A minute later, Hermione tested the knob, the door wasn't even locked. "I guess they don't get many visitors being this deep in The Forest."

She poked her head inside the door and looked around. No one was in sight. So she stepped in, with Harry and Ron following. There was a hall to the left and another to the right. She quietly crept down the hall to the left and poked her head into a red-carpeted music room with a piano and a harp. She headed for the next door and found a beautiful great ballroom. Still no one was around. Nearby were two bathrooms. The next door led to a kitchen, where elves were busy at work. She carefully closed the door, and backed down the hallway to the entrance hall. She tried the other hall on the right. She admired a giant tapestry hanging there. The old tapestry depicted wizards fighting giants. She opened a door and found the library. It wasn't empty. There was a man there, whom none of them had ever seen before. Harry recognized the strange position the man was sitting in. He had his legs crossed in the lotus position. The man was doing yoga! His eyes were closed in a meditative trance. Then, he spoke in a dreamy far away voice, "Next year's Super Bowl winner will be the NY Giants."

Hermione looked at Harry. Harry looked at Ron. Ron looked at Hermione.

The man continued a moment later saying, "Ron is wearing pink underwear with white bunnies."

"AM NOT!" yelled Ron. The man only continued to breath shallowly. Ron looked at Harry and Hermione and said, "He's lying!"

"Invest in plastics, it's the wave of the future."

Hermione took out her notebook and started writing, "Ooooh, this could be very educational!"

Ron looked worried, "You aren't going to write down that bit about my underwear? Are you?"

Hermione replied, "No, of course not."

"Hold on, I'll be right back," said Ron, and he dashed out of the room.

"Before the sun sets, Harry Putter will die!" said the strange man.

"Oh, great, someone else predicting my death, and yet, here I am still alive. Idiot!" said Harry indignantly. Hermione wrote it down.

"A chance meeting opens new doors to success and friendship."

"So, did you write down the part about Ron's underwear?"

"Uh, huh."

"Do you recognize this guy?" asked Harry.

"No," replied Hermione, "do you?"

"No."

"There is prospect of a thrilling time ahead for you."

"I think we should go get a cow, I can't figure out this weirdo," said Harry.

"Place special emphasis on old friendships."

Ron dashed in holding a half-gallon of chocolate chip ice cream, his weapon of choice. He cracked the man over the head with it. "That should shut him up!"

"Ron! I'm surprised at you!" said Harry. "Was THAT really necessary?"

"No, but it felt good," Ron shrugged.

Harry thought, "Now Hermione's violent tendencies are making Ron violent, too. Why can't we all just get along in peace and harmony, the way nature intended?"

They made their way out the backdoor, through the extensive gardens, through the field to the ranch house. Ron grabbed a rope. They rustled a steer from the corral. Ron put his wand in his robe pocket for safekeeping while he tied the rope around the steer's neck. When he was finished, he noticed the steer was chewing on the end of his wand.

"Oh, great, there goes another one," he sighed.

They led the steer around the house, through the gate, and through the Forbidden Forest of Sure Death toward Hogwashes.

As they walked, Harry asked, "So who do you suppose that millionaire guy with the mansion is? And why the cheesecake? It's got to have something to do with the Chamber of Cheesecake doesn't it? I mean, it can't just be a coincidence, can it?"

Ron shrugged stupidly.

"It's very curious, isn't it?" replied Hermione. "And these cattle aren't dairy cows, either. They have nothing to do with cheesecake. And just one more thing, those kitchen-elves weren't making cheesecake."

Millionaire business mogul, the reclusive Dr. Sherlock, world-renown for his food preparation factory's line of Dr. Sherlock Cheesecakes, the creamiest cheesecakes known to mankind, said, "Ow," and slumped to the floor of his mansion's library.

A week and a half later, Hasbeen had the second worst Friday the Thirteenth ever. Three hundred and fifteen hungry giant spiders showed up at three in the afternoon at his cabin door and were greatly disappointed.

Chapter 14

Guardians of the Cheesecakes

When they finally got the steer back to the Nerd House common room, it was just after dusk and time for dinner. Ginny Cheesley noticed them and asked, "Hey, what's that thing for?"

Ron replied, "We're gonna put it in Largebottom's bed tonight. Boy, won't he be in for a surprise when he pulls back his sheets tomorrow morning!"

"Whoo hoo hoo! It'll be a classic; won't Fred and George be proud!"

Hermione, Harry, and Ron left the steer in the Nerd House common room, where it went unnoticed for several hours.

They had dinner in the Great Eatery. Ron wrote a note to his mother:

> *Please send more wands.*
> *Love,*
> *Ron*

"I can't believe I'm out again already."

Later that night when most of the Nerds were asleep they met in the common room again, to finally make their attempt to get past the guard poodle and into the Chamber of Cheesecakes. A few Nerd students were up late watching Star Trek on the television in the Nerd House common room. When they saw Harry, Ron, and Hermione leading a cow out, they just figured the three were up to their usual hijinx.

The special cloak of Harry's was nowhere big enough to cover the cow so they left it behind. In fact, they had become so accustomed to sneaking around after curfew, that they were becoming more and more negligent. Harry completely forgot to check the Malarkey map before they left. He was too lazy to go back for it, so he sent Ron to peek around corners to see if anyone was there, before they brought the cow.

On the third floor, a suit of armor jumped down in front of them and lifting its visor, revealing custodian Gretchen Shoemacher. She had them caught red-handed. "Ah hah!" she cried out. "I've got you! Now you are going to finally get what's coming to you! You sneaky kids think you can fool me, but not THIS time. This time, you're gonna get yours! THIS time..."

Both Harry and Ron pulled out their wands and yelled, "Stupidify!"

Harry's spell of course stunned Shoemacher, who flopped forward with a loud crash.

Ron's broken wand fizzled and caused gravity to reverse. Everyone nearby instantly catapulted to the ceiling. Harry, Ron, and Hermione sat up, groaning. Harry was rubbing his neck. Hermione had both hands on top of her head. Ron was rolling on the ceiling holding his arm. In his fall, his wand became further broken. The steer was lolling loudly, and sprang up from the unfortunate Shoemacher who had broken its fall and was now unconscious. Hermione pulled a gauntlet off from Shoemacher, checked for a pulse, then said, "She probably would have died had she not been wearing that suit of armor. I think she'll be alright."

"Hermione, look at her face! Her nose has fallen off!" said Ron with disgust.

Hermione grabbed the nose and examined it. "It's rubber."

She removed the helmet from Shoemacher's head, with it came the woman's hair.

"It's a wig!"

Harry pointed, "That's not a woman. It's Belch!"

Ron asked, "What's Belch doing outta the hospital wing?"

Hermione asked, "Why's he dressed like a woman?"

"Maybe he's the Heir of the Err," suggested Ron.

"He must be!" Harry concluded. "No one could be that stupid!"

"He must have faked his own cheesecake attack! Why would he do that?" asked Hermione.

"To make sure no one would suspect him as the Heir of the Err!" she answered herself. "Harry, did you ever search the hospital wing?"

"No! I never bothered to look for a recipe book there!"

"Well, that proves it then! What do we do now?" asked Ron.

"We have the cow, we may as well see what's in the Chamber of Cheesecakes. Let's get going!" said Harry, leading the cow along the ceiling.

They led the cow up a flight of stairs using the underside of the stairs. They cast levitation spells to get to areas they couldn't normally reach from the ceiling. Then, on the fifth floor, they spotted Professor Ape patrolling the corridors, looking for a chance to subtract points from anyone who wasn't a PRK. He heard the echoing clunking of the cow's hooves. Ape looked all around for the mysterious source of the noise, but he never looked up.

"Putter, I know that's you! Putter!" He started groping around as though trying to locate an invisible object. As they continued past Ape high above on the ceiling, they could hear him yelling,

"Putter, I'll get you if it's the last thing I do!" Then he ran off, probably to wake up Grumblesnore.

When they reached the sixth floor ceiling, they kept levitating themselves and the steer up to the floor, until the anti-gravity spell finally wore off. When it did, they rolled over and stood up.

"What a relief to have my feet back on the ground," said Hermione.

They opened the door to the room with Skippy the poodle, and pushed the steer in. When the horrible carnage began, they ran through the room, lifted the trapdoor, and revealed a chute. Harry threw caution to the wind, and slid down it. He was deposited on an old mattress. Hermione and Ron were right behind him. Ron's wand snapped in a third spot as he landed. He tossed it away.

Harry and Hermione lit up their wands by reciting the spell, "G.E., we bring good things to life." They blinked until they became accustomed to the new illumination, and took in their surroundings. They were at the end of a secret passage. They followed it until they came to the other end, where there was a door. Harry opened it. There was a hallway on the other side, lit by torches. Harry noticed the hallway was blocked just ahead of them by the red and white striped wooden bar of a tollbooth gate. A loud growling snore could be heard coming from the tollbooth.

"What's a tollbooth doing in the middle of a secret passage?" asked Ron quietly.

"More important, what's making all that noise?" whispered Hermione.

They peeked in through the window of the tollbooth. It was occupied by a fearsome creature. It had the hindquarters of a lion, the wings of a bird, and the face of a woman. Her sharp teeth became momentarily exposed each time she loudly inhaled.

"That's the ugliest toll collector I've ever seen," whispered Ron.

"I saw an uglier one once in New Jersey," replied Hermione. "But that's besides the point."

"That's the sphinx," Harry said quietly. "It's the same one I met during the Fry-Wizard Tournament."

"The sphinx is a rare and intelligent creature," began Hermione. "It asks you a riddle, and if you can't answer it, it eats you. The first person to answer the Riddle of the Sphinx and survive was Theseus of the Greeks. Harry is the only other person I've ever heard of that encountered a sphinx, solved her riddle, and lived."

"That doesn't sound like something I want to face, should we jump over the bar?" asked Ron.

"Can you jump that high, Ron?" asked Hermione.

"I think so," whispered Ron.

"Give it a shot, let's see if it works," encouraged Harry.

Ron readied himself for the attempt, then dashed forward gaining momentum as he ran down the passage. When he reached the bar, he sprang. He got enough height that his lead foot cleared the tollbooth bar, however, his back foot didn't clear and he ended up landing face first on the stone floor with a quiet thud. A loud alarm rang on the tollbooth wall, waking the sphinx. She quickly turned the annoying alarm off.

The sphinx yawned and stretched, then casually put her head out of the tollbooth. "Oh great, more children. Isn't that just stellar. Here I am, most formidable guardian known to mankind, protecting some supposedly hugely important treasure room, from what? Kids. I could be replaced by a childproof cabinet latch. I tell you anyone of intelligence would be depressed, and here I am with an IQ way off the charts, and a brain the size of Zion. It's enough to make me want to quit this cushy little job, and I only have three more months until I can retire and collect my pension."

She paused to look at the three children. "This is the part where you make sympathetic noises."

"Aw, poor thing!"

"Tsk, tsk, how horrible."

"Ow, I dink I broke my nose."

"Too little, too late," the sphinx sighed.

"Maybe you really should quit?" Harry said hopefully.

"Say, I remember you, you're Harry Putter. Back again, eh? Say, can I get your autograph this time? Not for myself of course, I got two little monstrosities at home. And I'm not just saying that, they really are hideous."

"Sure," Harry obliged. Using his quill, Harry signed two dried out bones for the sphinx. Hermione, Ron, and Harry all wondered if the bones were human bones.

"Excellent, you're easily my best adversary of the day."

"So, we're the only ones so far then, right?" asked Hermione.

"My, my, you are an exception, aren't you? Well then, let's get down to business. Let me explain the rules." The sphinx cleared her throat, "Ahem. In order to pass, you must each answer the Riddle of the Sphinx. And your friends can't help you."

Hermione became nervous. "Oh, I'm so worried, what if I can't answer the question?"

"If you can't answer or you get the answer wrong, I throw a pie in your face, laugh at you, and send you back to your Common Room," answered the sphinx.

"Oh, what a relief, I thought you were going to eat us!" replied Hermione.

"Well, I'd really love to, but I've been instructed not to eat the students. So as disappointed as I know you must be, I'm afraid it's going to have to be pie."

"What kind of pie?" asked Ron. Hermione gave him a look.

"I prefer banana cream," replied the sphinx.

"Cool! I love banana cream, I'll go first," said Ron, licking his lips.

"Good luck, Ron," whispered Hermione.

"Very well. Your riddle is: where did you get the cow that you used to get past the poodle?"

"From the corral at the mansion in The Forbidden Forest of Sure Death."

Hermione was nervous for Ron. Was his answer good enough?

"Very well," said the sphinx. She pressed the button to raise the bar that blocked the dungeon hallway, "You may pass." Ron strolled past, and the gate lowered again.

"Holy Crap! That's easy! Harry, you made that Fry-wizard turny-thing sound tough. I can't believe I was worried. I'll go next," Hermione said, stepping forward.

"Very well, your riddle is: what is the annual rainfall of Muskogee, Oklahoma?" asked the sphinx.

Hermione's jaw dropped. Dumbfound, she blinked and muttered, "How should I know?" Very quickly she found herself in the Nerd House Common Room, her face covered in banana cream pie. The laughter of the sphinx ringing in her ears was quickly replaced by the laughter of the late-night Nerds surrounding her. She spat, stomped her foot, and said, "I hate banana cream pie."

"Oh, that's too bad," said the sphinx, "sorry about your friend with the big head."

Harry stepped up, "I'm ready for your question."

The sphinx said, "Your riddle is:

> A friend of yours has strange habits,
> one of them has to do with rabbits.
> If you were to go down under,
> it would certainly give you cause to wonder:
> Why would he wear his undergarments
> covered with the fuzzy varmints?
> But one question stands out above the others,
> Why would he wear underwear this color?

What color is it?"

Harry sighed, this was obviously a longer and more difficult riddle to solve. Well, he had no time to lose, he'd have to get started analyzing the riddle line by line.

He thought, "Hmmm, a friend of yours has strange habits. Well, Hermione and Ron are my best friends, and they both have some very strange habits. One of them has to do with rabbits. Neither Ron nor Hermione had a pet rabbit. Could it be someone else, some other friend with a rabbit? Perverti Pickle had a rabbit, but she's more of an acquaintance than a friend, and I think she said it died. I can't remember anyone else having one, except, Bingo! Humphrey the Wise and mystical has stage rabbits! Next line."

Just then Ron coughed to get his attention. He looked at Ron who was holding his hand up with all his fingers curled down, except his pinky finger, which was extended.

Harry looked puzzled.

Ron pointed at his pinky finger.

"Must Concentrate. Next line," Harry thought. "If you were to go down under. Australia? What does Australia have to do with me, I don't know anyone from down under. Or do I? Nope, I don't. Paul Hogan? Nah. Next line. It would certainly give you cause to wonder. I'll bet. Next line."

Just then, Ron started singing and strutting, "I'm coming up, so you better get this party started!" It was really distracting.

"Zip it, Ron, I'm trying to concentrate!"

He thought, "Next line. Why would he wear his undergarments. HIS! It had to be a guy. It couldn't be Hermione! It had to be Ron, Humphrey the Wise and Mystical, or Paul Hogan. Next line. Covered with the fuzzy varmints. Fuzzy varmints could be rabbits. Who did he know who had a rabbit? Ron had a rat, Scrabbles but

Scrabbles turned out to be Vermintail, a servant of the Fart Lord, and ran away, but rats ARE fuzzy varmints."

Another cough from Ron, caused Harry to look up again. This time Ron had his pants down, and was waving his butt around.

"Cripes, Ron, quit it! How am I supposed to solve this riddle when you keep acting like a complete idiot!"

"Next line. But one question stands out above the others, leading to the final question, why would he wear underwear this color? What color is it?"

Harry sighed, "Ron, do you know the answer?"

"I've been trying to tell you the answer for the past five minutes."

The sphinx interrupted, "No cheating! Your friend can't tell you the answer!"

"Can he give me a hint?" asked Harry.

"Well, I suppose, you are Harry Putter after all, we can't expect you to stick entirely to the rules," conceded the sphinx.

Ron asked Harry, "Remember that weirdo in the mansion?"

"Yeah."

"He made a prediction, remember?"

"Yeah, the next super bowl winner will be the NY Giants. I already called my bookie and placed a ten galley bet on 'em."

Ron buried his face in his hands, "Keep going."

"Something about plastic."

"Keep going."

"Ron Cheesley wears pink fuzzy bunny underwear."

"Yes!"

The sphinx hit the button and the bar raised to let Harry Putter walk past. She chuckled to herself as Harry and his friend walked down the hall into the next room. Then she slapped her paw on the intercom button and said, "This is Ernie calling Bert, come in Bert. Over."

A moment later, "Bert," buzzed in, "Bert here. Yes?"

"Target has just passed checkpoint B. Over."

"Excellent! Good job, Ernie."

"Really? You think so? Well, I can't tell you how much that means to me. Hearing you say that, well, it really makes my day! What a rewarding experience this job has been. So much opportunity for personal growth. Why, I tell you…"

Ron and Harry walked down the hall into the next room, where the next cunningly devised trap awaited all who might attempt to gain entrance to the Chamber of Cheesecakes. They entered the Bingo Hall. Inside there were many people who had made it this far in their endeavor to reach the elusive room of cheesecakes. Those who had braved the peril of Skippy the Poodle, and correctly answered the Riddle of the Sphinx, now sat around with numbered cards in front of them, waiting for the next number to be called. Some of them were skeletons covered with cobwebs. Some of them were asleep. They spotted their roommates, Spleen Davis and Shameonus Finnigan. Professor McGooglesnot was also there, playing nine cards and smoking like a fiend.

A ghost that Harry and Ron had never seen before was calling out the numbers cried out, "B1." McGooglesnot covered B1 on two of her cards with a chuckle.

Harry went to the pile of cards, and searched for ones that had B1 on it, he took one for himself, and one for Ron, and grabbed some bingo chips, waiting for the next number to be called out.

"N34," called the ghost. Neither of them had N34 on their cards.

"What are we doing?" whispered Ron.

"Playing bingo," Harry whispered back.

"I know, but why?"

"It must be our next test. If we can win, maybe we can move on."

"O67"

Ron covered O67 on his card then waited for the next number.

"Z194"

"Z194? That's not a real bingo number!" Ron complained loudly.

"Hush up, Cheesley, I want to hear the next number!" retorted Professor McGooglesnot.

"YY39,189"

"Harry, I think this is going to be a long game," said Ron looking around the room. "How can we speed this up?"

"Let's cheat!" whispered Harry.

Ron and Harry pulled out their quills, and as the ghost called each number, they wrote them down on their bingo card in a row. On the fourth call, they each wrote down PPP4,367,147 and cried out, "BINGO!"

Professor McGooglesnot scowled, "Beginner's luck."

The ghost came over and checked their cards, and declared them winners. They were allowed to pass through the next door.

They followed the corridor beyond the Bingo Hall. There were no doors to either side, and very soon they came to a yellow wall of cheese blocking the way.

"That's odd, you don't see a wall made of cheese everyday," said Harry.

"I hope this means we're getting close to the Chamber of Cheesecakes," Ron replied.

"What kind is it?"

Ron put his nose up to it and smelled. "I think it's mozzarella! My favorite! I'll eat the whole thing. But when he tried to gouge a piece from the wall with his finger, he couldn't.

"Try to take a bite, but be careful, don't break your teeth."

Ron tried to take a bite gingerly. His teeth sunk into the cheese, where his fingers couldn't. He chewed a bit. "Yuck, it's cheddar!" He tried to spit it out, but couldn't, he had to swallow it.

"Start eating your way through."

"Why do I have to eat it? Why can't you?"

"Well, you are a Cheesley after all, aren't you?"

Forty-five minutes later Ron clutched his full and extended belly and groaned again. "Ugggh, I can't go on! I'm stuffed. I can't even move." It was his third time stopping, only this time, he sat down, and leaned against the wall of cheese.

"Come on, Ron, you're almost done," pleaded Harry.

"Ugggh! Harry, you'll have to go on alone. I can't make the hole big enough for me. You'll have to squeeze through the hole I made. I think it's big enough for you, you're skinnier than I am."

Harry looked at poor Ron, he looked almost green from eating so much cheddar cheese. "Don't worry Ron, I'll send for help once I get out of here."

"Good luck, Harry!"

It was a tight squeeze, but Harry made it through.

Chapter 15

The Chamber of Cheesecakes

On the other side of the cheese wall the air was dark and cool. Harry, alone now, lit up his wand once more, and then followed the passage to another door. He opened it wondering what he would have to face next, a dragon perhaps?

No. There was no dragon inside the tackily decorated room. The room was oriental in style, with rice paper walls and plastic flowers in large vases. It was illuminated by intricately painted paper lanterns. The furniture looked like it was from the seventies. There was a couch, two chairs, and a coffee table in one section. The other side of the room was a kitchen nook. The little kitchen had a table and a counter with a sink and a coffee maker. Under the counter there was a mini refrigerator. Nearby, was a water cooler. There was also a door, opposite Harry. However, no cheesecakes were in sight. Harry started for the refrigerator.

Suddenly two large ninjas burst through the rice paper walls, one of them expertly swinging nunchucks, the other drawing knives.

"Gulp, Ron? Hermione?"

Then a third and smaller ninja burst through another rice paper screen. He was holding a spear.

"Neville?"

The two big ninjas started to laugh. Harry thought he had heard that laugh before. Then the smaller ninja pointed at him and said, "Looks like we have you now, Putter!"

It was the voice of Faco Maldoy!

"Faco! Shabby! Foil!"

"None other! Surrender Putter, or prepare to duel!"

"Don't you mean prepare to die?" asked Harry, his wand at the ready.

"Die, Putter? Do you know how much trouble we'd be in, if we killed you? Don't be stupid! Hey, guys, let's shave his head bald!" replied Faco. Shabby and Foil laughed.

"You'll do no such thing, boys," sneered Carnivorous Ape as he appeared in the doorway opposite. "Good work boys, you finally caught him. That's an extra twenty points for the PRKs. Now, it's time for you to hit the Jacuzzi. Head back to the PRK spa room."

The three PRKs headed for the door behind Ape. Harry started to follow.

"Not you, PUTTER!" yelled Ape. He paused, then said, "Well, well, well, it looks like you've really stuck your neck out this time, Putter. You put it right on the chopping block, and now you're going to be expelled!" Ape laughed. "Hand me your wand, Putter!" He held out his hand, expecting Harry to give it up peacefully.

Harry had no choice, he had to hand over his wand to Ape. He regretfully surrendered it.

"And I might add, it has been a long time coming." Ape sneered. "You see, Putter, you never learn! You don't know how predictable you have become. The Fart Lord trapped you last year using your uncle as bait, and you predictably ran to the rescue. It gave me an idea, Harry, a way to get rid of you. Yes, Harry, I loathe you. I hate you because you are the son of James Putter."

Harry interrupted, "You hate me because my father treated you like …like… dirt when you were both students?"

"At first, yes, but it's more than that now. Like your father you never follow the rules either. Rule and laws are there so that we can all enjoy the same rights and privileges as each other, without endangering each other, hurting each other, or killing each other. Your father had no respect for the rules, and neither do you. You think you're special! Above the law. You are cheating scum, and yet people love you for it. That's the rub! It's just not right! They should hate you for the juvenile delinquent that you are! You are no better than a hoodlum. If we all followed your lead, Putter, we might as well flush society down the toilet where it would belong. We could all live like animals, doing whatever felt best at the moment. Take for example the Chamber of Cheesecakes, if this really was a Chamber of Cheesecakes, what would you have done with ..."

Harry interrupted again, "Wait a sec, 'if this really was a Chamber of Cheesecakes?' What does that mean? This can't be it?"

"Poor confused boy. No, Putter, you see, I trapped you. I made up the Chamber of Cheesecakes. I bought a Dr Sherlock's cheesecake. I made a sign. I made up a mystery. One that you simply couldn't resist. So, no Harry, there is no Chamber of Cheesecakes, no Err of Slipperin, only a boy in a room he shouldn't be in if he followed the rules. You are so predictable, Putter."

"So the guard dog, the riddle, the bingo game, and the wall of cheese all guard ... nothing?" asked Harry.

"The teacher's lounge," said Ape, holding his hand up, indicating the room they were in.

Harry was having a bit of trouble catching up to the reality of the situation.

Belch walked in through the door behind Ape. He was still wearing the suit of armor. "Harry Putter, Ha, HA! Looks like you finally caught him, Professor! Thank God." Belch started doing a little victory dance. "Finally, I can stop wearing that stupid dress."

Ape smiled, "And now Harry, you've broken your probation, and Grumblesnore will have no choice but to expel you. Good riddance to bad rubbish."

"Grumblesnore won't …"

Ape snapped, "He most certainly will! You'll see! There you go again, expecting to be treated special! You are not special! You are just like everyone else, Putter, and when you or anyone else breaks the rules, there are consequences and repercussions!"

Harry protested, "Well, we'll just see about that! Let's go talk to Grumblesnore! I bet he'll have you sacked once he finds out about your evil little plot! You're sick, you are. All those children suffering, just so you could catch me. It's sick I tell you."

Ape laughed, "Children suffering? Do you honestly think we would hurt the other students? Stories, Harry. All stories. The reason you don't know any of the children who were attacked, is because we made them all up. I also think you will be quite surprised to know that Grumblesnore is in on the whole thing. It was his guard dog, his sphinx, his bingo game, and his wall of cheese. You see, Putter, Grumblesnore has had five years, six if you count preschool, of trying to run a school with you around, and like me, he is quite sick of it, too."

"So you three conspired to get rid of me this year!"

"Yes, Putter, and if I'm not mistaken, Grumblesnore will be here very shortly to say goodbye, and I'm sure he will be in a very good mood."

"You're insane, Ape," came a voice from behind one of the rice paper screens. It was the voice of Gildersneeze Farthard, yet he sounded different somehow. Harry breathed a sigh of relief. Gildersneeze would save him from Professor Ape. Harry knew everything would be all right.

Farthard burst into the room destroying another rice paper wall. "If you think I'm going to let you expel Harry, you missed your path in life. You should have been a jester! Harry is a celebrity among wizards, not only has he on several occasions defeated He-Who-Must-Not-Be-Smelled, but he has won dozens of quibbage matches, and the Fry-Wizard Tournament. Harry's fame has been spreading throughout the world like wildfire. And Hogwashes is making a KILLING selling Harry Putter books, T-shirts, toys, and other promotional merchandise."

Harry smiled. He wondered, what happened to Farthard's lisp? He wasn't drooling either.

"I can't expel him, can't I? You overstep your bounds, Farthard! Harry has been breaking the rules ever since he got here. He's on probation, and I've caught him red-handed out of his room past curfew, and in a restricted area! Grumblesnore will have no other choice but to expel the brat! Furthermore, Hogwashes does not receive any commission on all the Harry Putter merchandise being sold around the world, you imbecile!" said Ape with detestation in his voice. He never could stand Farthard, the bumbling idiot.

"Well, if you really insist, be my guest. You can expel him after I'm through killing him!" An evil sneer twisted the face of Farthard.

Harry's smile vanished. "Kill me? But why?"

Ape stared at Farthard too, wondering why the fool, Farthard, would want Harry dead, and how the idiot thought he would accomplish it with Ape right there to prevent him from doing it.

"Ape, Ape, Ape, I fear I am quite beyond your comprehension," chuckled Gildersneeze. "But you, I understand all too well. Treacherous men are ever distrustful. But you needn't fear for your own skin. I do not wish to harm you, as you would know, if you really knew me. So I am giving you a final chance. You can leave Harry to me, of your own free will, –should you choose to. But first, you will surrender your wand. It shall be a pledge of your conduct, to be returned later, should you merit its return."

"Surrender my wand, and you call me the jester? Farthard, you are indeed a moron. Harry, come with me, we'll go talk to Grumblesnore, –in private."

In a sharply commanding voice, Farthard rebuked Ape, "I did not give you leave to go. I am not finished. You are a fool Ape, and yet pitiable. You might yet have turned from your folly, and been of service. But you choose to gnaw the remains of your old plot, when a new one is afoot."

Ape was astonished. Gildersneeze spoke, and Ape found himself obeying. This was not the drooling idiot, Farthard. Something was indeed afoot.

"Behold," said Farthard, "I am not Gildersneeze Farthard, whom you call moron and imbecile. I am Gandulf the Off-White, who has returned from slumber." He removed the illusion disguising himself as Farthard. It was Gandulf the Off-White.

"Holy Crap!" said Carnivorous Ape.

Belch turned to run, but was quickly catatonic, as Gandulf cast a stupidifying spell on the school custodian. He fell to the ground with a crash of armor.

"Ape, your wand is broken." At Gandalf's words there was a crack, and the wand split asunder in Ape's hand, and fell down at his own feet.

Harry was remarkably calm. "But why, Gandulf? Why would you want to kill me? And why now?"

"Now? Hmmpf, foolish boy, I've been trying to kill you all year. Wasn't it becoming obvious with each deadly creature I released upon you in class? And why do I want you dead? Isn't that obvious too? I've been the most famous wizard for decades, until this young upstart fledgling of a wizard, Putter, turns up selling more books and merchandise that I have in nearly fifty years on top! And let me tell you, you've accomplished nothing, boy! All the wizards in this tale are wimps compared to me and the powerful wizards I've had to deal with. And you haven't brought a single one down! As a matter of fact, you've let Lord Fartypants grow more powerful in each book I've read so far. And let me tell you, if there ever was a chump of a wizard, it's the Fart Lord. Please, I could make him lick my boot! But anyway, it's time to put an end to this charade and my competition. I will be the greatest wizard once again! Nothing personal, Putter."

Harry had a lot more questions, but a voice came from behind another one of the rice paper screens. "A chump, am I? Gandulf, you overestimate your own powers. Sure you killed the ballrog, but it took you what? Three days? And if it weren't the luck of those lembas-eating midget friends of yours, you'd have been squashed by Saurun. We all read the books. The elf, Legollas, was way cooler than you!" said Lord Moldyfart as he burst into the room.

"Lord Moldyfart," Gandulf sneered.

"Yes, indeed. And if anyone is going to kill Harry Putter, it's going to be ..."

"ME!" interrupted yet another voice from behind yet another rice paper wall. From behind the screen, Elvis Grumblesnore stepped through the paper wall and into the room.

"For fifty years, I run a school peacefully and like clockwork, then Harry Putter shows up, and for the past five years, six if you include preschool, it's been nothing but trouble, danger, and a huge mess! All my problems will be gone, once and for all, when I kill Harry Putter!"

Harry's jaw dropped. "Not Grumblesnore too," he thought.

"So now it's 'kill' is it? Not expel?" asked Ape.

"Sorry, Professor, if I don't do it, one of these two will. And I asked myself, do they really deserve to kill Harry? And I answered myself, no, I deserve to kill him. This may be my only chance."

"So, is everyone here then?" asked Ape.

"Not quite, ho, ho, ho," laughed a voice from behind yet another rice paper screen. The voice was unfamiliar.

"Now who can that be?" asked Gandulf, clearly becoming impatient as all these other wizards kept showing up all wanting a piece of Putter.

Santa Claus smashed through the rice paper screen in front of him, toting a sawed-off shotgun.

"Santa!" cried Harry, pinching himself. "Not you too? Why?"

"'Fraid, you forgot to leave out milk and cookies this Christmas," said Santa, matter-of-factly. "Just kidding, ho, ho, ho, I had a lot of money riding on that quibbage match last year, you stinkin' rotten cheater!"

"Santa," said Elvis Grumblesnore, "you don't have to deal with him everyday like I do, have pity on me. Why don't you go back to the North Pole and leave the wizard-slaying to those of us who really deserve to kill Putter?"

"Sorry, Grumblesnore, but where I come from, the guy with the bigger gun makes the rules, and unless you don't want any presents come Christmas, I suggest you go back to your office and be a good little boy!"

"So are we all here now?" asked Gandulf. Everyone's head turned to the only intact rice paper screen left. However, there was no reply.

Gandulf drew his sword, Spamdring, and ran it through the last paper screen and into the body of whomever it was standing behind it. He wrenched his sword from his victim, and stepped back as Ophelia's father, Polonius, fell through the rice paper screen and into the room.

Polonius cried out. "O, I am slain!"

At this point, Carnivorous Ape stepped in front of Harry and said, "Listen all of you, regardless of what you think, none of you are above the law. You just can't go around killing people. Besides, violence is the last resort of the incompetent."

Harry thought it was the bravest thing he ever heard. But when the other four trained their weapons on Carnivorous Ape and let loose, his body dropped half a second later, riddled with shot, seared with electricity, shriveled up in flames, and cursed to death, Harry turned white as a ghost! This was the most deadly group of adversaries ever assembled, and they meant business. If only there was some way he could get his wand back from the corpse of Ape. But if he tried, he knew he would be instantly killed. And even if he were to somehow get his wand, would it still be in working condition?

"So, how are we going to decide who gets to kill him?" asked Grumblesnore.

"Biggest gun!" growled Santa, as he pumped his smoking shotgun, automatically loading the next cartridge and expelling the spent one.

"Seniority," said Gandulf.

"Most powerful," said Moldyfart.

"How about a contest?" asked Elvis Grumblesnore.

"A contest?" they all asked together, including Harry.

"Yes, winner gets to kill Harry!"

"What form of contest?" asked Gandulf suspiciously.

"How about we all jump into Lake Iwannabealifeguard, the one who makes the biggest splash wins?" replied Elvis.

"What? At the same time?" asked Moldyfart.

"That is the most foolish contest I've ever heard of!" cried Gandulf, who couldn't swim.

"No, it's not, it's brilliant," exclaimed Santa, secretly thinking he had the meanest cannonball around.

"It's ingeniously clever, not one of us knows who would win such a contest," Lord Moldyfart thought aloud.

"If we want the outcome to be random, might we simply draw straws?" asked Gandulf, who was planning to cheat at drawing straws.

"BORING!" shouted Santa.

"If we do this contest, Grumblesnore, who would be the judge?" asked Moldyfart.

"Harry can be the judge!" said Grumblesnore.

"Putter?" sneered Moldyfart.

"Yes, Harry," said Grumblesnore firmly.

"Why not?" chuckled Santa.

And though they were supposedly some of the greatest thinking minds in the realm of fiction, none of them could indeed think of a reason why not.

They headed out of the teachers' lounge, out the backdoor of Hogwashes, and down to Lake Iwannabealifeguard. Then much to Santa's distaste, they drew straws to determine the jumping order. Gandulf cheated and got to go first. Santa would be second, followed by Moldyfart, then Grumblesnore. Gandulf nervously pulled an inner tube around his waist. He climbed the ladder. He looked at Harry to make sure he was watching, then he stepped to the end of the diving board, and did his best cannonball, causing an enormous splash that looked like giant horses. He hoped the boy liked horses. He felt rather proud of his work, and considered the inner tube a great way to keep it secret from the others that he couldn't swim. He paddled leisurely to the shore and climbed out. "Ha! Beat that, Nick!" Then he wiggled out of his inner tube as a giant squid wrapped a huge tentacle around him, and instantly pulled him to the depths below never to be seen again. Santa, Moldyfart, Grumblesnore, and Harry all stared at the ripples on the surface of the water.

"Wow," thought Harry, "Nemoy sure has grown!"

Moldyfart turned to Santa and said, "Right then, you're next!"

Santa gulped, "I hope that thing is full now." Santa laid his shotgun on one of the lounge chairs. He climbed onto the diving board, sprang up and down a few times to get momentum, then jumped, tucking his knees under his arms, somersaulting through the air. Meanwhile, Moldyfart and Grumblesnore gave each other a look, pulled out their wands, and said, "Use Glad freezer bags!" at the same time. The spells they cast instantly froze the surface of the lake solid. Santa hit the frozen lake top, and despite its thickness, he put several hairline cracks in its surface. The surface also put several hairline cracks in Santa's skull.

"Very naughty, boys!" said Santa just before he fell unconscious.

Grumblesnore slashed out with his wand, saying "Wigwamia Levi-Straussa!" and he levitated Santa's bulky body off the ice, and placed him in a nearby lounge chair. Then stabbed with his wand at the lake saying, "Hunka Hunka Burnin' Love" and the lake surface instantly became water once again. He turned to Moldyfart and said, "You're up!"

"Just how stupid do you think I am?" asked Moldyfart. "You'd better give me your wand first. I'm not going to let you cast any spells at me while I'm diving."

"And what, you think I'm just going to hand my wand over to you?" snorted Grumblesnore.

Moldyfart started to object, but Grumblesnore held up his hand for quiet. "The solution seems to me, that I will give Harry my wand to hold while you dive, so that I can't interrupt you, and in turn, you will give Harry your wand to hold as I dive. Will that be alright with you?"

Moldyfart conceded that the plan would work, so long as Grumblesnore was disarmed during his own dive, and Harry couldn't escape. The boy was helpless, he couldn't use another wizard's wand, and somewhere deep inside the school, that sniveling fool Ape's now cold corpse still held Harry's wand. The boy couldn't abbarate, couldn't attack, couldn't defend himself, and couldn't run away. He was helpless.

Grumblesnore handed Harry his wand. Then Lord Moldyfart climbed up on the diving board, and did a cannonball that sent a tremendous splash into the air.

"Wow," said Grumblesnore, "that's going to be tough to beat."

Harry decided to make a run for it. He ran as fast as he could, but Lord Moldyfart surfaced, and flicking his wand at Harry, said the magic words, "Keeanu Reeves!" It was one of the unforgettable curses. Harry found it far worse than the Nicole Kidman curse. His body instantly became wracked with pains, as though he was being forced to actually watch a Keanu Reeves performance. He flopped to the ground and starting rolling in agony. It was the same curse that had put Neville Largebottom's parents in the insane asylum. Even if he didn't go insane, Harry would never again be able to look upon Keanu Reeves's likeness without getting the willies.

Moldyfart stepped out of the lake, snapping his wand upward. Harry felt instantly relieved. "What a simpleton!" said Moldyfart. "I knew the idiot would try to make a break for it. Grumblesnore, you had better not let him get away, or I'll kill YOU instead!"

Grumblesnore said, "I'm sure Harry won't want a second helping! Make no mistake, that's just what you will get, if you try that again, boy!" Grumblesnore dragged Harry by his robes back to the lakeshore roughly. He retrieved his wand from Harry, and waited for Moldyfart to relinquish his own wand temporarily for Putter to hold as Grumblesnore dived.

But just before he handed his wand over, Moldyfart became suspicious. "How do I know you two aren't trying to trick me?" he asked himself aloud. "Yes, I see, you disarm me, and then turn sides again, Grumblesnore, killing me instead of Harry! I've figured out your little plan!"

"I give you my solemn word, that I will not attack you. In fact, I regret all my past endeavors to prevent you from killing the boy. I have indeed have had a change of heart."

"Your solemn word? I'm sorry, but that just won't do! I've given mine many a time, and it turns out that dead men don't question you after you've taken it back. No, I think a little insurance is what's needed here!" said the Fart Lord. Then he readied himself to cast a summoning spell. With the magic words, "Swanson's Hungry-Beast Dinners," two slavering bandersnatches appeared out of thin air.

"You, keep your eyes on this boy, if he attempts to run, you are to rip him to shreds and eat him," commanded He-Who-Must-Not-Be-Smelled.

The deadly creature grinned devilishly.

Then Lord Moldyfart turned to the other bandersnatch, and said, "You, keep a close eye on this one. He will be diving in the water, follow him, should he at any moment, before he enters the water or after, reach into his pocket, make him your midnight snack!"

The feral creature's eyes gleamed with expectation.

"There! Now I can turn my wand over to Putter, and still be quite safe," said the Fart Lord triumphantly as he handed over his wand to Harry.

"A bit paranoid are we?" asked Grumblesnore, who didn't seem even a bit nervous under the careful observation of the beastly creature. He was of course very careful however, to keep his hands away from his pockets.

"Never trust an enemy, Elvis," Lord Moldyfart retorted. "And now, I believe it is time for the contest to resume."

Grumblesnore climbed onto the diving board, the bandersnatch following. He wasn't nervous as he sprang, somersaulting twice before hitting the water with a splash as large as Moldyfart's. The bandersnatch jumped in behind him.

When he surfaced, Moldyfart said, "Nice try, Grumblesnore, but I win!"

Elvis scrambled out of the lake, as he tilted his head trying to knock water out of his ears. The creature continued to follow him observing him closely. "What was that, Moldyfart? I'm afraid I couldn't hear you properly with all that water in my ears."

Lord Moldyfart recovered his wand, grabbing it from Putter's hand, "Give me that!" Then turning back to Grumblesnore, "I said, 'Nice try, but I win!'"

"Not so fast, Moldyfart! Harry is the judge. Harry?"

"Looked like a tie to me," said Harry as he casually stepped over to the lounge chair and picked up Santa's shotgun. He blew the nearest of the two bandersnatches to kingdom come.

Grumblesnore started to reach for his wand, but just as suddenly stopped, realizing in the nick of time that the remaining bandersnatch was still guarding him closely.

The Fart Lord however, trained his wand on Putter. Putter ignored him, pumping the shotgun, automatically expelling the spent cartridge, while loading the next. Moldyfart yelled, "Ina Godda Da Vida, baby!" The death curse. However, the spell didn't produce the desired effect. Moldyfart looked down at his wand. "What the?" he said, realizing that it wasn't his wand after all. It was a fake. He flinched as the next shotgun blast blew the remaining bandersnatch away.

Grumblesnore, no longer under the watchful eye of the slavering beast, finally pulled out his own wand. "Darn it!" he said. His wand too, was a fake. He threw it in the lake.

Harry snickered and held out their real wands.

"This is all your fault, you idiot!" yelled Moldyfart. He turned and gave the old schoolmaster a punch in the nose. Grumblesnore fell down in a heap from the blow, unconscious.

Then he turned back to Harry, "I can't believe it! Three wizards of far greater power than you, plus Santa with a shotgun. There is no reason why you shouldn't be dead right now! But, Nooooo, Harry Putter never loses! You may have gotten away this time, Putter, but I'll be back. Next time, you won't be so lucky. You are still no match for me!"

Harry said, "Sayonara Sucker!" as he pumped the shotgun. Then, he pulled the trigger and blew the Fart Lord away.

He lowered the shotgun. He had done it. He had finally finished Lord Moldyfart off once and for all. In the end, either Harry had to kill Lord Moldyfart, or Lord Moldyfart had to kill Harry. What a relief that it was all over. Perhaps now, he would stop having adventures. He could just be a normal kid. He could finish school, grow up, find a girlfriend, get a job, and maybe even one day, get married.

He looked over at Santa. He was still breathing, but Santa had hit his head pretty hard, he'll need to see Nurse Pomfrite. Grumblesnore, too, was breathing, his nose bleeding. Grumblesnore would need to visit the hospital wing, too. The bandersnatches were gone; they had disappeared back to where ever they had come from. Lord Moldyfart was breathing too. In fact, to Harry's astonishment, he rolled over and stood up slowly.

Harry's jaw dropped. He wanted to ask how it was possible, but all he could manage to say was, "But …."

"Nice try, fool, but you can't kill me that way!" laughed the Fart Lord. "You'll never defeat me, Putter, not until pigs fly! Because you don't know the one Word of Power that would change me back to my true form for all eternity." Moldyfart laughed again evilly.

"Cripes! Really?"

"You see," began Lord Moldyfart, "What?" His body began to smoke. Harry just stared.

"No one uses that word! IT"S NOT POSSIBLE!" he yelled. He began to scream, "NOOOOOOOOOOOO!!!!" Billowing smoke hid the Fart Lord from view as he metamorphosized into his true form. Lord Moldyfart was a groundysnout. He snorted in disgust and flew away.

Chapter 16

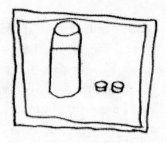

The Hospital Wing
Revisited

Elvis Grumblesnore was lying in bed in a private room in the school's hospital wing. His nose had been broken the night before by Lord Moldyfart. Nurse Pomfrite had put a bandage on it, more to cover where his skin had been split open, than to do anything to make it better. The slave-elf, Bobby, stood on his bed holding up a hand mirror. Elvis looked in the mirror at his now gruesome face. Both of his eyes had been severely blackened by the blow. It was all Harry's fault. He was in a foul mood, when in walked Harry Putter to visit him, carrying a bouquet of flowers. (Harry had scoffed them from a vase in one of the school portraits. The woman in the portrait had been pretty mad about it, but her feelings weren't important to Harry, as she couldn't do anything to Harry about it.)

Harry said, "Good morning!"

Grumblesnore rolled his eyes and said grumpily, "I don't see what's so good about it. As a matter of fact, it seems to be going downhill rather rapidly." Bobby frowned, and climbed down from the bed, standing quietly at his master's side, should he be needed.

"Grumblesnore, I want to thank you for saving my life!" Harry said handing the flowers to the headmaster. "That was an ingenious plan you had last night to trick Moldyfart and all the others. I was almost convinced that you really wanted to kill me, until you set up Lord Moldyfart like that!" Harry laughed. "Then I realized that he's never going to be a match for you! You're far too brilliant a wizard, you fooled them all."

Then Harry became more serious as he sat on the edge of Grumblesnore's bed, and said in a lowered voice, "I'm sorry I ever considered not coming to school this year. I promise no matter what, no matter how many people want to kill me, I'll always trust you to protect me, and come here, where I belong."

Bobby slapped his own forehead, but said nothing.

Grumblesnore chuckled, then said sweetly, "Oh, Harry! You're the real genius! You see through all my tricks. Even the wall of cheese, which I must say, was one of my most brilliant ideas to date. What? What? A wall that you had to eat through, impossible to eat any cheesecake after that! How is Ron by the way? Has he recovered from eating all that cheese?"

"Nurse Pomfrite says he's pretty backed up, but he'll be fine in a couple of days."

"And Santa? He hit his head pretty hard. Is he alright?"

"Yes, Nurse Pomfrite healed his fractures already, and he said he's planning to take off a year to recover in Cancun! He's borrowed Hasbeen to take over his duties until after next Christmas! He said Hasbeen seems to have a knack for handling magic reindeer. So Hasbeen's going to be delivering all the presents this year!"

Grumblesnore was turning more and more red as Harry spoke, until he exploded, "What! He can't do that! He's needed here! Who's going to take care of the Magical Petting Zoo? I can't do everything! Who allowed this to happen?"

"Santa, Hasbeen, and I arranged the whole thing earlier this morning."

Grumblesnore's eyes narrowed, "This was your idea, wasn't it?"

"Well, it was the least I could do, you should have seen how happy Santa was with the idea. And with Hasbeen in charge, I'll bet we get everything that we ask for!" said Harry delighted.

Grumblesnore was far less than delighted. "You idiot! You're ruining my life!" He grabbed Harry by his pencil-like neck and started to choke him.

"And you are completely wrong about me, Harry! I wasn't acting like I wanted to kill you! You've been nothing but trouble since you first came here, and you've made my life a MISERABLE HEADACHE! Killing you will solve all my problems at once, and maybe after next Christmas my life will start to get back to normal! Instead of dealing with The Demented running around the school, and evil wizards, and getting the sack, maybe I will be able to run a school for a change!"

Harry's face was starting to turn blue, he couldn't reply, he had to do something, he was running out of breath. But he couldn't loosen the grip of Grumblesnore's claw like hands around his throat. Then suddenly, the headmaster let go.

"Nurse Pomfrite," said Grumblesnore, trying to sound innocent. "I didn't see you there! I was just trying to help Harry get an eyelash out of his eye!"

Harry was gasping for breath.

Nurse Pomfrite said, "I brought you some ibuprofen, Grumblesnore, I heard you yell that you have a miserable headache." She handed him the tablets and a glass of water.

"Thank you, my dear, that was very thoughtful of you to anticipate my needs. But, I hate to take you away from your other patients."

"Well, I suppose I'd better check and see how Cheesley is doing," she replied and started heading out the door.

"Wait!" yelled Harry. "I'll go too! I want to see how Ron's doing!"

Grumblesnore pleaded sweetly, "Stay with me a while longer, Harry!" He smiled at Nurse Pomfrite as he held his water in one hand, and grabbed Harry by the shirt collar with his other, the ibuprofen falling somewhere onto his bed.

"But visiting hours are over! Aren't they Ms. Pomfrite?" croaked Harry, as he twisted trying to get away. He considered telling Ms. Pomfrite the truth, but he knew she would never believe him.

She turned and said, "Oh, you can stay for five more minutes. It won't kill anybody." Nurse Pomfrite left, and Grumblesnore's smile left with her.

"Okay, but I can only stay for five more minutes. What time do you have?" asked Harry.

Grumblesnore sighed as he turned his wrist to look at his watch, accidentally spilling the glass of water in his hand directly onto Bobby the house-elf's head. Bobby immediately transformed into a sharp-toothed fiend, and starting biting and scratching Grumblesnore in a way that reminded Harry of the Tasmanian Devil from Loony-Tune Cartoons. Grumblesnore lost his grip on Harry's collar.

Harry ran from the room, to the screams of Grumblesnore, "You did that on purpose! You'll pay for this!"

Harry closed the door, and flipped the sign hanging on the knob so that it read, "Do Not Disturb!"

Chapter 17

The Last Day
of School

Professor McGooglesnot stood up in front of the entire school body in the Great Eatery. Only two people weren't there. Grumblesnore was still recovering from the mysterious accident that incapacitated him several months ago. Professor Ape wasn't nearly so fortunate, he had died from his extensive injuries. Rumor had it, they had suffered grievous injuries while fighting a terrible beast, rescuing Professor McGooglesnot and several students, and closing the Chamber of Cheesecakes forever. Supporting this rumor was the fact that there had been no mysterious cheesecake incidents since.

Professor Ape's death greatly affected Harry. It was the third death surrounding him in the past three years. The first was Cedric Biggleby. Cedric had died during the Fry-Wizard tournament. Along with Harry, he was trapped by the Fungus Eaters. In order to restore their master, Lord Moldyfart to his full powers, the Fungus Eaters killed Cedric. Harry battled the Fart Lord and escaped. The second death was Serious Smack the Clown, Harry's elusive uncle, who had died in the bizarre circus tragedy last year. Ape was the third, the most recent, and the closest yet to Harry.

While Harry hardly knew Cedric or Serious Smack the Clown, he knew Professor Ape very well. And it was only now that he was dead that Harry realized just how well. He had been spending hours each day with the Professor during Poisons class, and immediately after practicing yoga. He realized that Ape had tried to teach him some very important lessons: the importance of peace; the value of obeying rules and laws; and that violence is the last resort of the incompetent. And only now that Ape was dead, did the lessons finally make sense to Harry. So he did the only thing he could. In the memory of Ape, Harry took his lessons to heart.

The next time Hermione attempted to swat an elf. Harry masterfully stayed her hand. He commanded the elf, "Your services are not wanted here. Go, and do not return."

The elf wordlessly obeyed.

Ron got up to leave too, before he realized Harry wasn't talking to him.

Hermione was more than impressed. Harry had changed, and she liked it. She asked him to sit next to her on the submarine ride to Atlantis. Of course, he said he would.

A month later, Yu Rang broke up with Michael Coronary. Soon after, Yu Rang approached Harry and groaned a deep guttural growl. Harry gracefully apologized, and explained that he had already made other plans for the submarine ride to Atlantis. Yu Rang moaned in dismay.

The trip to Atlantis had almost been a disaster. When the submarine surfaced in Lake Iwannabealifeguard, a giant squid started wrestling with it. The squid was as big as the submarine. It looked like the trip was going to be canceled for sure, when Ron stepped forward and commanded Nemoy to release the vessel. Everyone was amazed when the squid listened to Ron.

The trip was saved. There were no further incidents after that, and the trip ended up being wonderful. It was the highlight of their school year.

Hermione never parted sides from Harry. Not at the Neptune Museum, the King's Palace, the Atlantic Aquarium, or at the Coliseum. They even sat next to each other at The Ambergris Grill, where Harry felt comfortable enough ordering cheesecake for dessert. His choice caused quite a stir among the other sixth year students.

"Well, it has been a very studious year. I'm very pleased to see how much everyone has learned. Headmaster Grumblesnore would be proud of you all. Unfortunately, he cannot be here to congratulate the winners of this year's House Cup in person. However, he has asked me to assure you that he is very pleased with all of his students, and wishes you all a pleasant summer. He asks you all to use your break to have plenty of fun, enjoy yourself, and to get all your silly shenanigans and other malarkey out of the way, because they'll be none of that come next term. He looks forward to seeing you all next year. I'd like to congratulate you all on his behalf." McGooglesnot paused to a brief smattering of applause.

"Now, without further adieu, it is an honor for me to present the House Cup to this year's winners." At this, the audience began to show some excitement, especially the Party Animals, where many a catcall rang out.

"In fourth place, the Jock House with a score of 55 points." There was a round of polite applause.

"In third place, the Par-tay Animal House, scoring 60 points. The Party Animals erupted in huge applause including wolf-whistles and shouts of "DUDE!"

When the uproar died down, McGooglesnot continued, "In second place, the Popular Rich Kids, scoring 75 points." The end of her sentence was drowned out by groans of dismay as everyone realized the Nerds had won yet again.

"And in first place, the Nerd House, with a new point total record of 246, 885 points!" There was a smattering of polite applause and the noise of much goofy laughing and celebration. Neville Largebottom became so excited, he had to use his asthma inhaler.

"We also had a new personal point total record. Hermione Stranger with a total of 246, 875 points!" The Nerds all cheered again for Hermione.

Professor McGooglesnot clapped her hands, and a truly magnificent feast magically appeared in front of them all. The food was incredible, after having subsisting for so long on Henry the Kitchen-Elf's slop all through the year. They all began to feast merrily.

Then a small girl stood up on one of the Party Animal tables and yelled, "FOOD FIGHT!" She lobbed a handful of mashed potatoes at Ron Cheesley. Her accuracy was to be admired. She had bright orange hair. It was little Suzanne Cheesley.

Ron couldn't control himself. He grabbed a handful of cranberry sauce and flung it at his sister. He hit Charlie Cartuffle by mistake.

Ron ignored the food being thrown in his direction from several others, as he took aim at Suzanne again this time with a bowl of applesauce. Suzanne danced down the row of Party Animal tables, and jumped down. Ron ended up splattering Ella Mentry and Athena Stalebread with it by mistake.

Ron snatched at anything. He was being pummeled by all kinds of food. Suzanne climbed up on the teachers' table.

Ron adjusted his aim to account for Suzanne's momentum as she cartwheeled down the length of the teachers' table. Then he threw. The huge glob of cheesecake he had grabbed arced through the air toward where his target would be in a moment, when all of a sudden Suzanne stopped. The cheesecake sailed by her and made a terrific splat as it landed in Professor McGooglesnot's face. Minerva was much impressed with the consistency of the cheesecake, or at least the small portion of which had inadvertently splattered into her open mouth. She smiled; it had been a long time coming.

The food fight that ensued was astronomic in proportion to the one of the preceding year, making it far and away, the worst or greatest one ever, depending on one's point of view.

Hours late, because the students were forced to clean up the largely destroyed Great Eatery, they finally boarded the train back to London. Harry, Hermione, Ron, Ginny, and Suzanne shared a train compartment.

Harry handed Suzanne a folded linen sheet and a battered scroll of parchment. He said, "I decided a while ago that it was time for me to pass these on to someone else. I've been trying to decide who I'd like to give them to for quite some time now. And I just decided who I want to have them."

"Me?"

"Yes, you Suzanne."

He taught her how to use the Malarkey Map and the special cloak.

"You're certain you won't need 'em any more?"

"Certain? No, but I have a strong feeling I won't."

"Harry, Mom was wondering if you'd like to stay at the Boil for the summer?" asked Ron.

"Hmmm, that does sound like fun! Let me call Aunt Hachooie and find out if it's alright with her."

He pulled out his cell phone and pressed the speed-dial number for home.

"Aunt Hachooie, hi, it's me, Harry."

"Harry Putter, your nephew," he paused.

"I want to know if it's alright with you and Uncle Vermin, if I stay the summer at the Cheesleys?" He suddenly jerked the cell phone away from his ear.

Ron distinctly heard the minute sound of cheering.

"Hello? Great! Thanks, Aunt Hachooie!"

The End

Printed in the United States
80720LV00004B/80